The Graphic Novel

Sleeping Beauty

RETOLD BY MARTIN POWELL

ILLUSTRATED BY
SEAN DIETRICH

Graphic Spin is published by Stone Arch Books,
A Capstone Imprint
1710 Roe Crest Drive
North Mankato, Minnesota 56003
www.capstonepub.com

Library of Congress Cataloging-in-Publication Data
Powell, Martin.
    Sleeping Beauty / by Martin Powell; illustrated by Sean Dietrich.
    p. cm.   (Graphic Spin)
    ISBN 978-1-4342-1193-4 (library binding)
    ISBN 978-1-4342-1393-8 (pbk.)
    1. Graphic novels. [1. Graphic novels. 2. Fairy tales. 3. Folklore.] I. Dietrich, Sean, ill.
II. Sleeping Beauty. English. III. Title.
PZ7.7.P69Sl 2009
741.5'973 dc22   2008032048

Summary: Once upon a time, an evil fairy cursed a young princess. On her fifteenth birthday, the
princess pricked her finger on a spindle and fell into a spell of sleep. Trapped behind poisonous
thorns and guarded by deadly zombies, only the bravest soul can awaken her. Otherwise, she will live
forever in eternal slumber.

Creative Director: Heather Kindseth
Graphic Designer: Brann Garvey

Printed in the United States of America in North Mankato, Minnesota.
062013   007392R

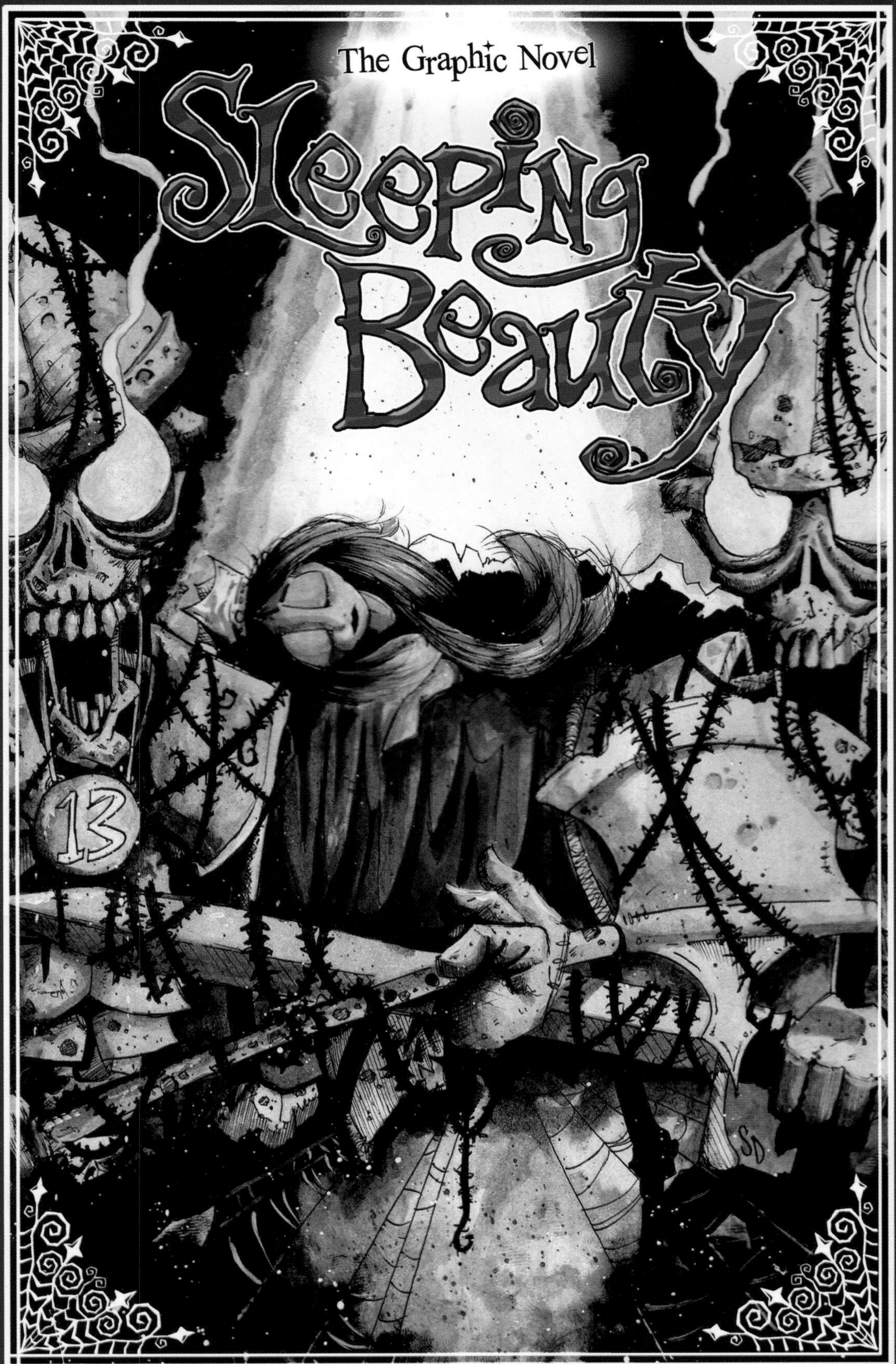
The Graphic Novel
Sleeping Beauty
13
SD

Cast of Characters

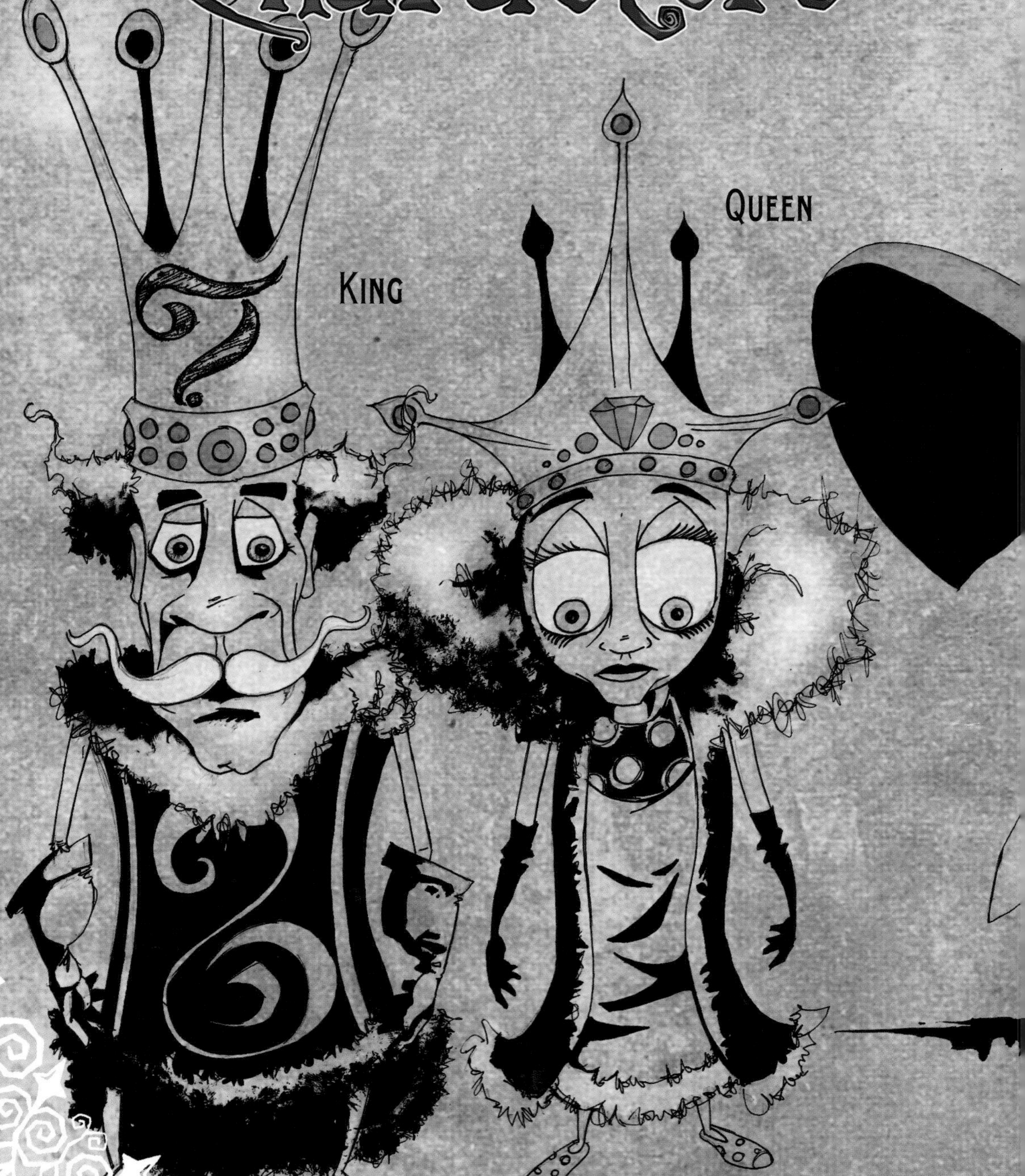

King
Queen

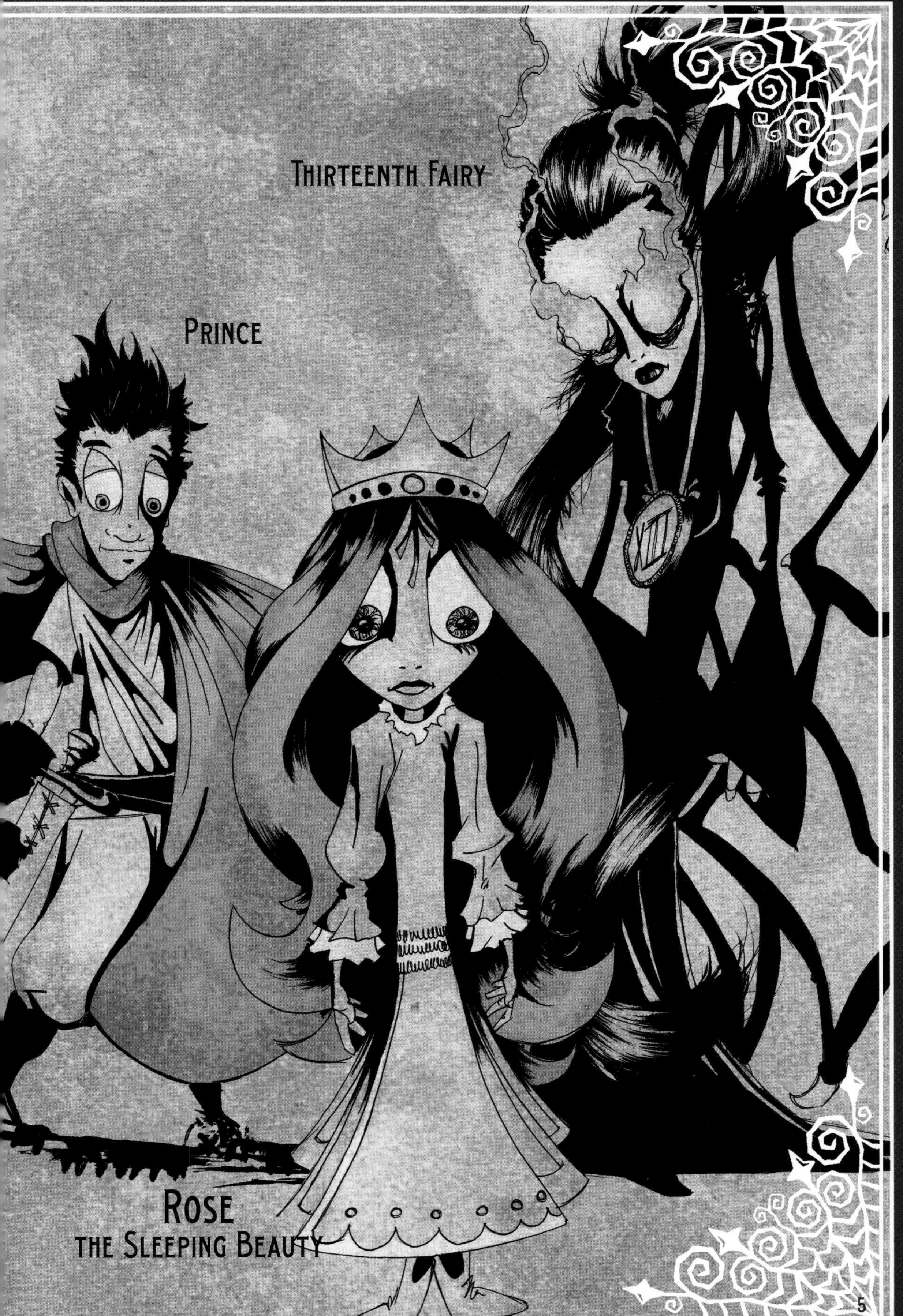
Thirteenth Fairy
Prince
Rose
the Sleeping Beauty

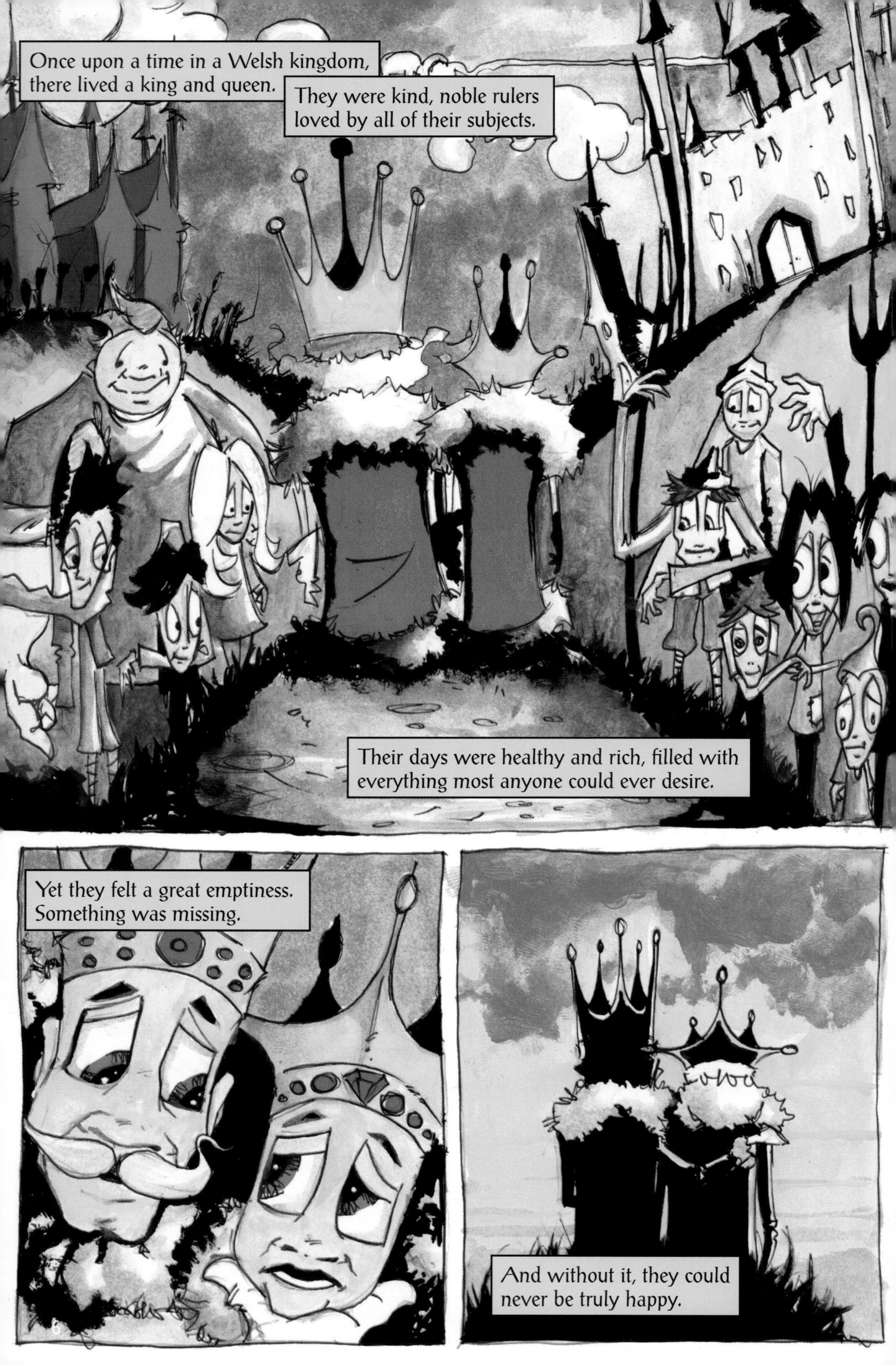
Once upon a time in a Welsh kingdom, there lived a king and queen.
They were kind, noble rulers loved by all of their subjects.
Their days were healthy and rich, filled with everything most anyone could ever desire.
Yet they felt a great emptiness. Something was missing.
And without it, they could never be truly happy.

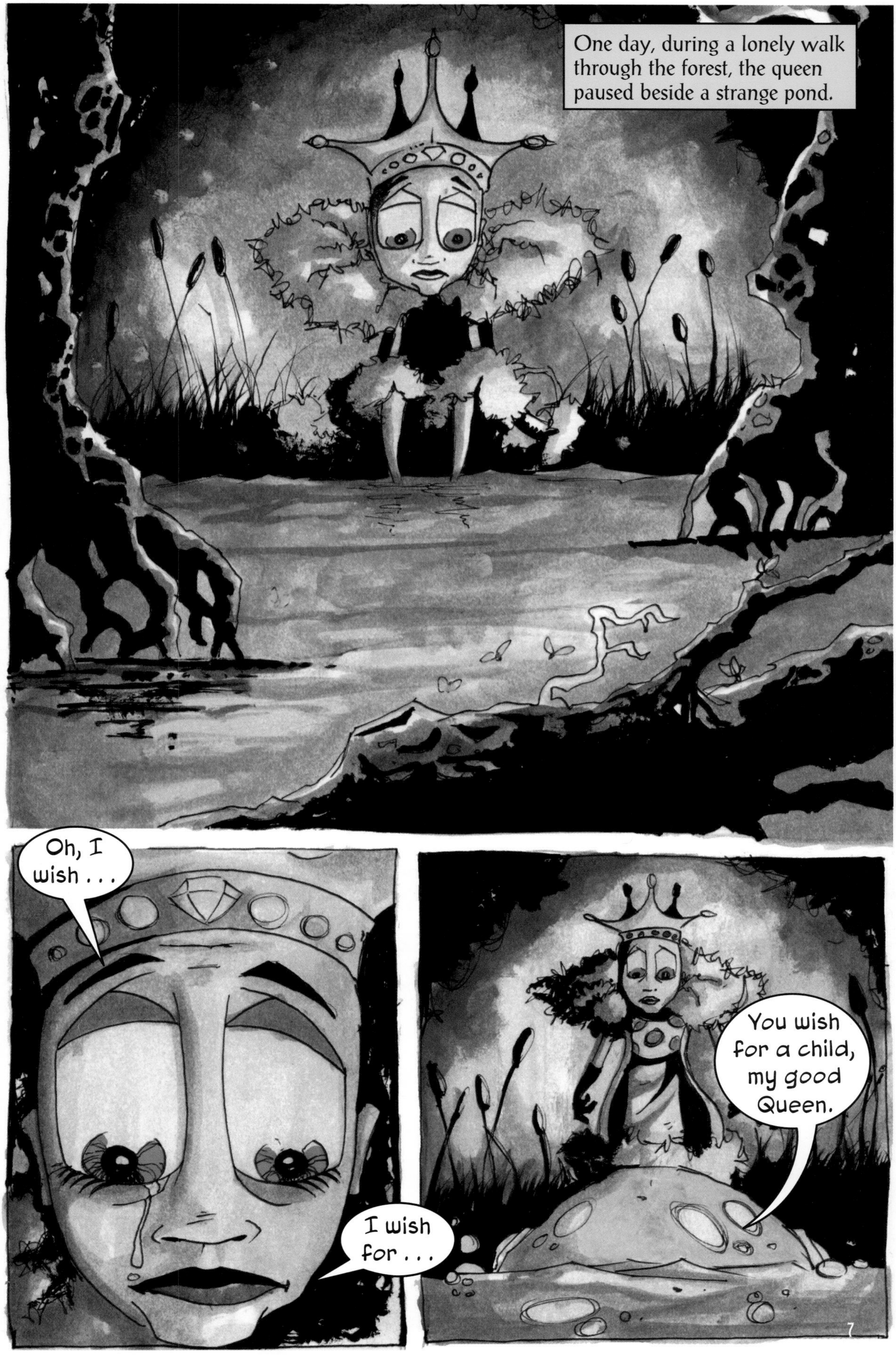

One day, during a lonely walk through the forest, the queen paused beside a strange pond.
Oh, I wish . . .
I wish for . . .
You wish for a child, my good Queen.

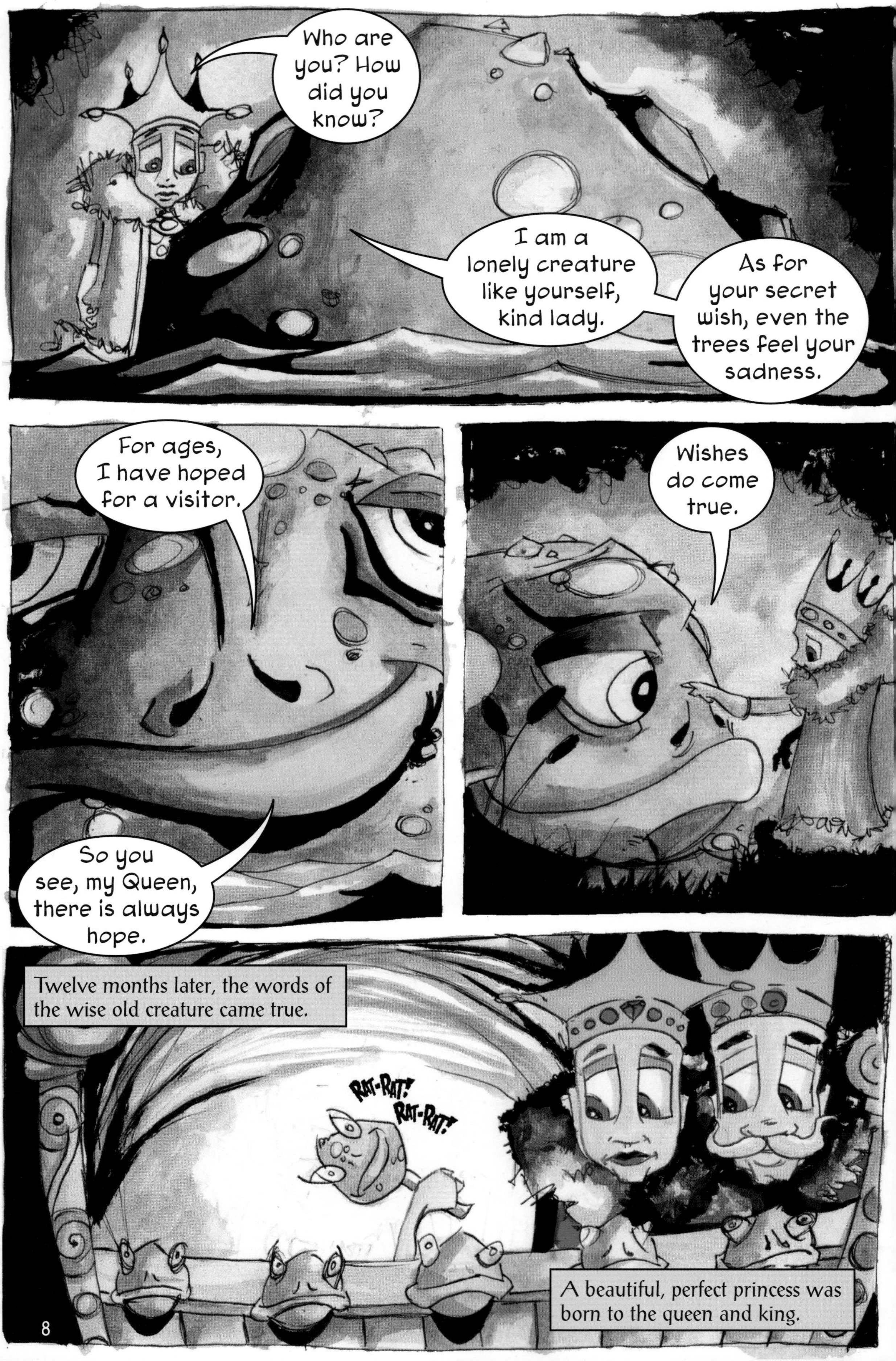
Who are you? How did you know?
I am a lonely creature like yourself, kind lady.
As for your secret wish, even the trees feel your sadness.
For ages, I have hoped for a visitor.
So you see, my Queen, there is always hope.
Wishes do come true.
Twelve months later, the words of the wise old creature came true.
RAT-RAT! RAT-RAT!
A beautiful, perfect princess was born to the queen and king.

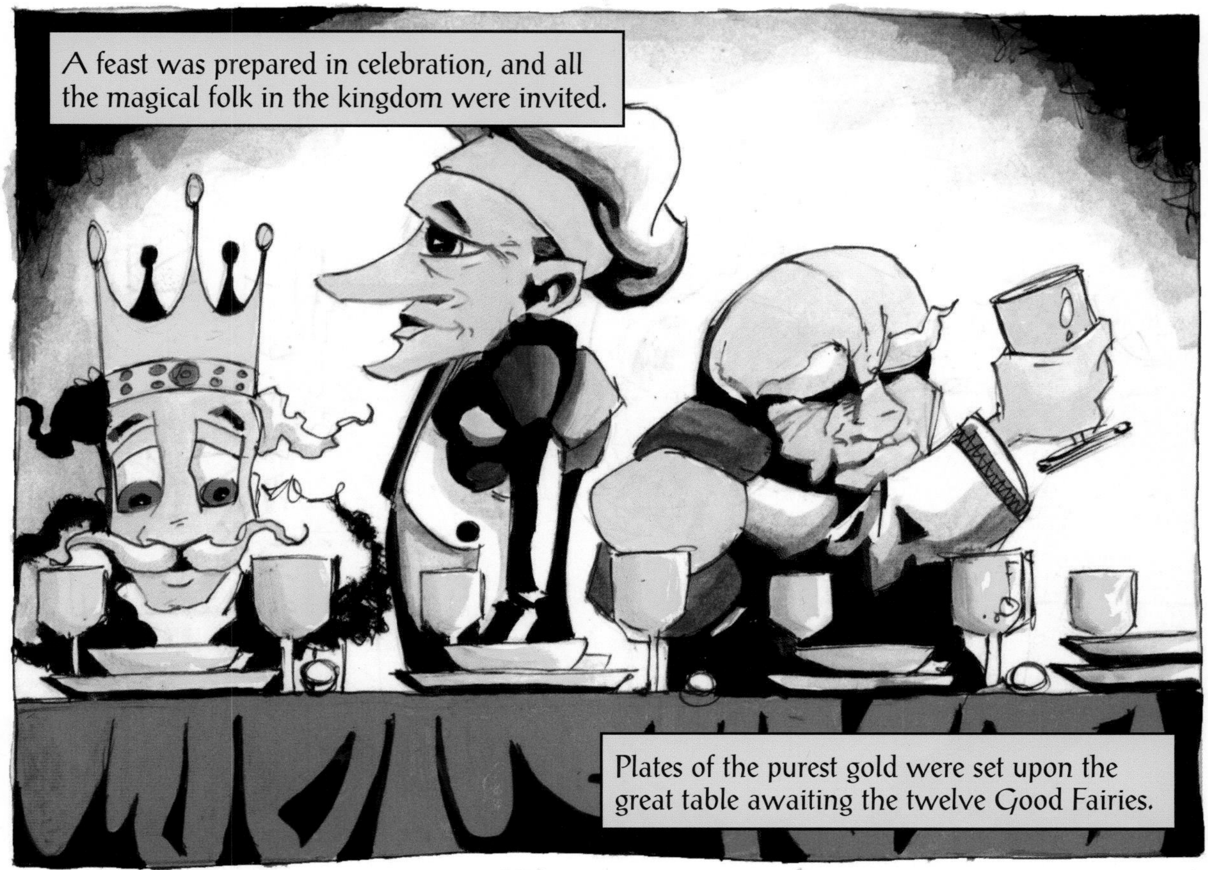
A feast was prepared in celebration, and all the magical folk in the kingdom were invited.
Plates of the purest gold were set upon the great table awaiting the twelve Good Fairies.

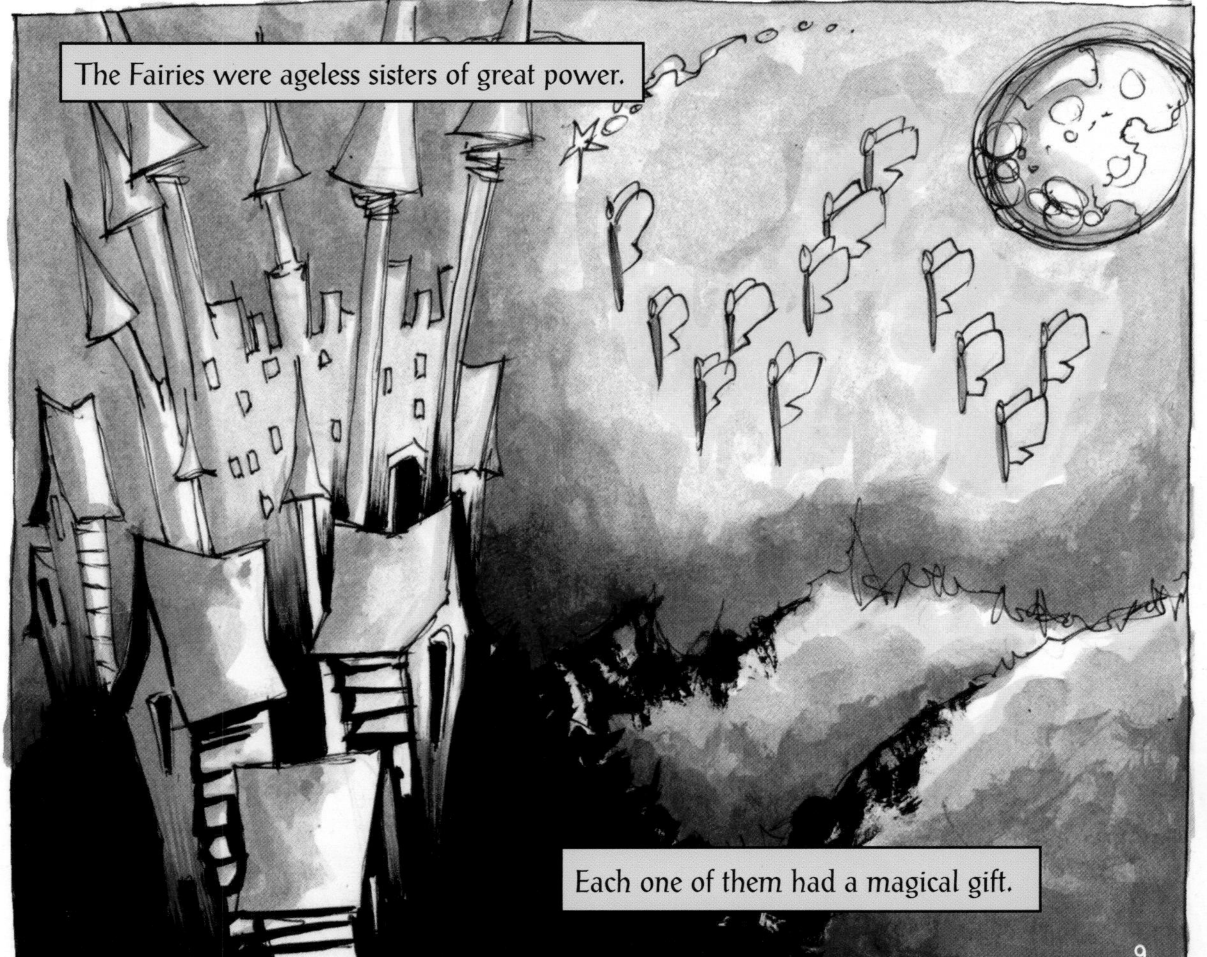
The Fairies were ageless sisters of great power.
Each one of them had a magical gift.

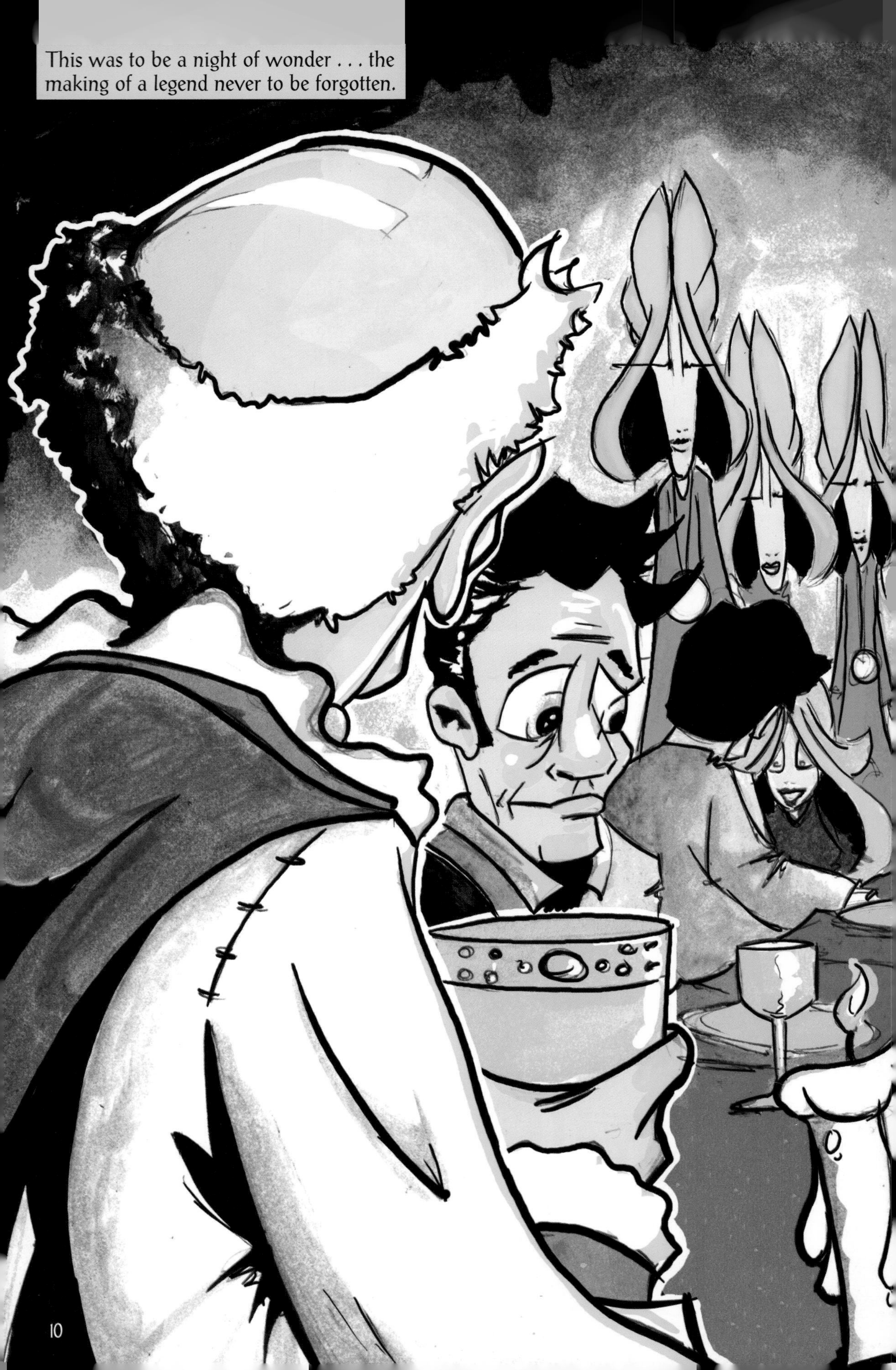
This was to be a night of wonder . . . the making of a legend never to be forgotten.

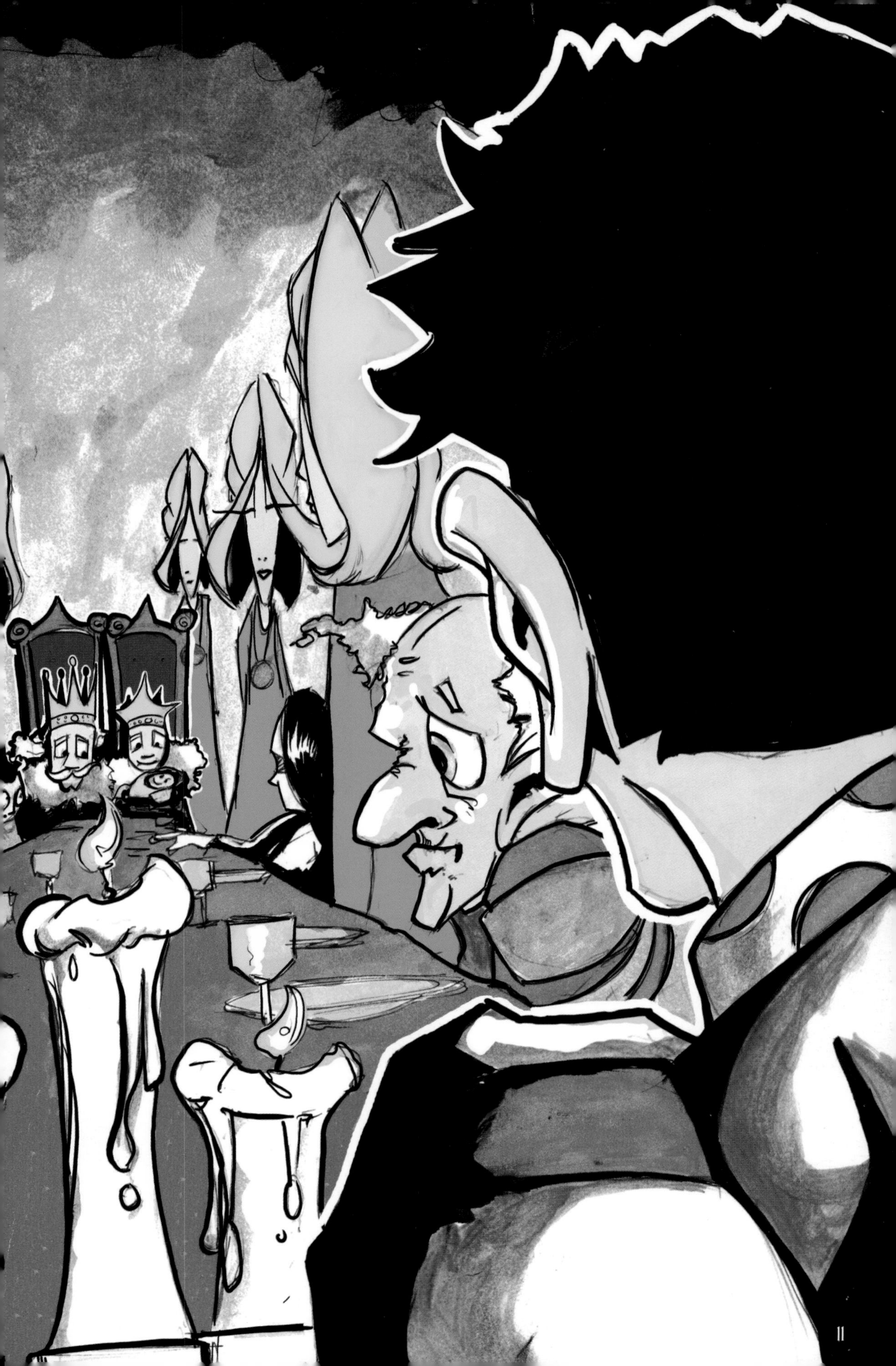

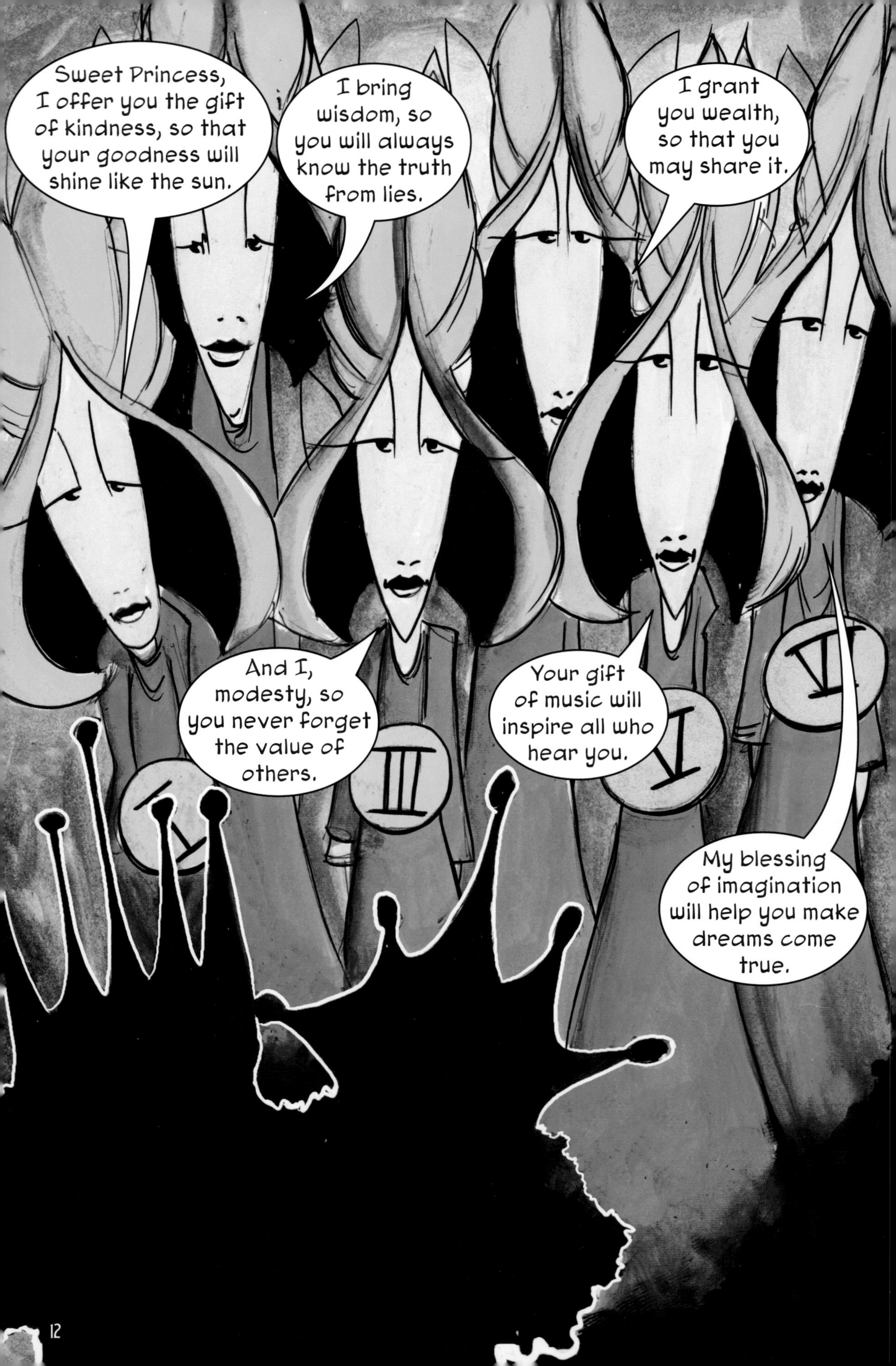
Sweet Princess, I offer you the gift of kindness, so that your goodness will shine like the sun.
I bring wisdom, so you will always know the truth from lies.
I grant you wealth, so that you may share it.
And I, modesty, so you never forget the value of others.
Your gift of music will inspire all who hear you.
My blessing of imagination will help you make dreams come true.

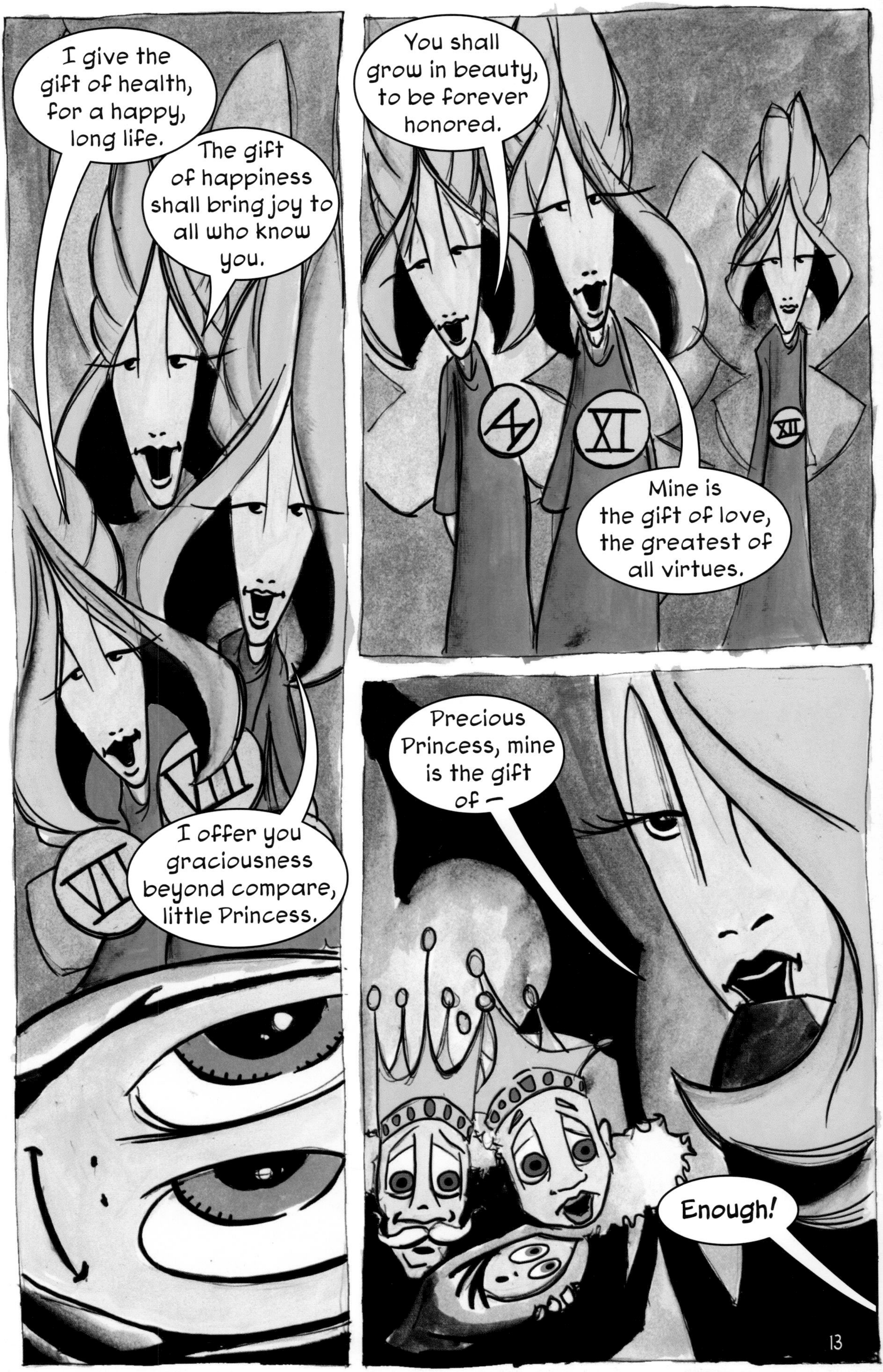
I give the gift of health, for a happy, long life.
The gift of happiness shall bring joy to all who know you.
I offer you graciousness beyond compare, little Princess.
You shall grow in beauty, to be forever honored.
Mine is the gift of love, the greatest of all virtues.
Precious Princess, mine is the gift of —
Enough!

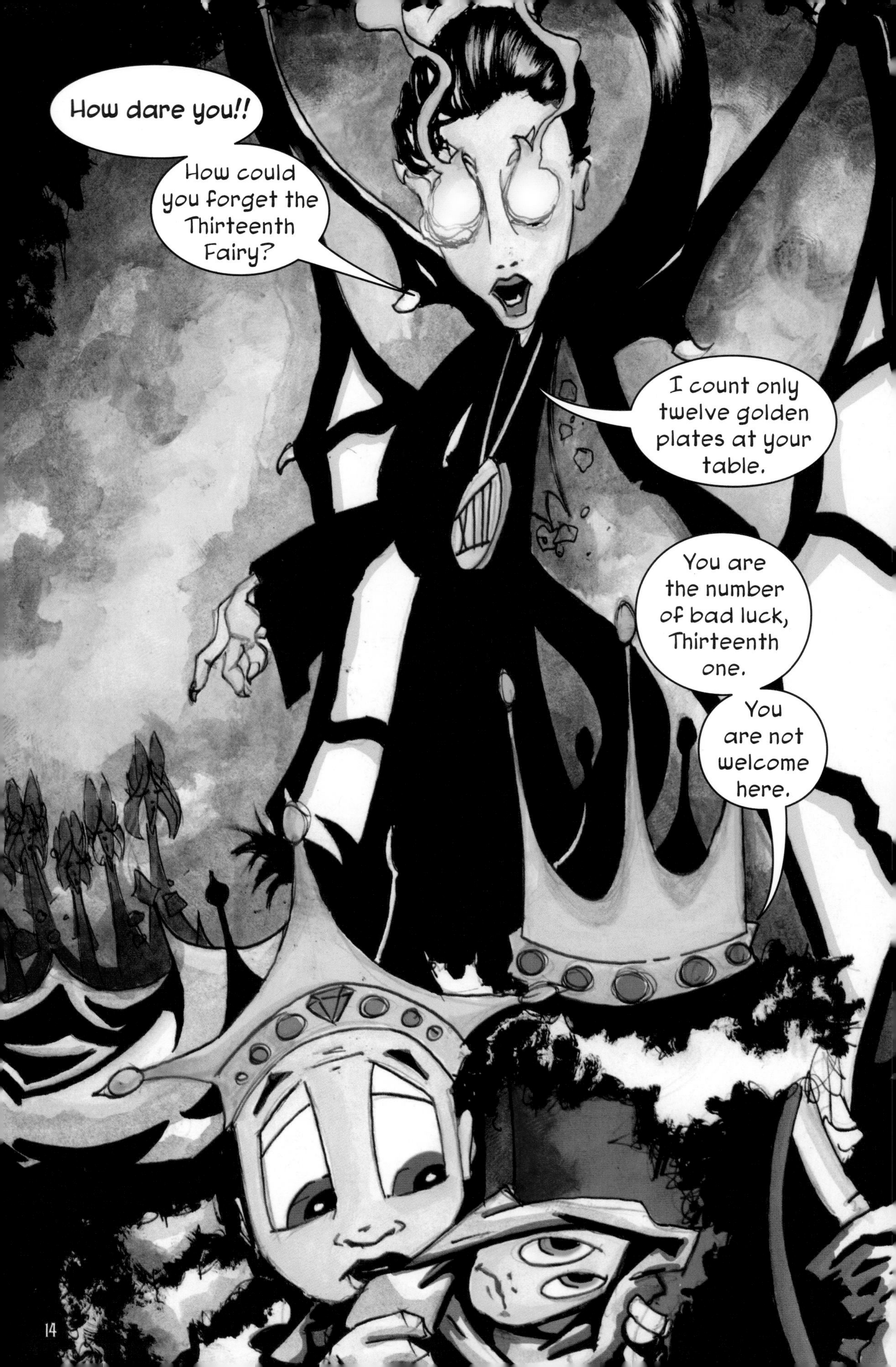

How dare you!!
How could you forget the Thirteenth Fairy?
I count only twelve golden plates at your table.
You are the number of bad luck, Thirteenth one.
You are not welcome here.

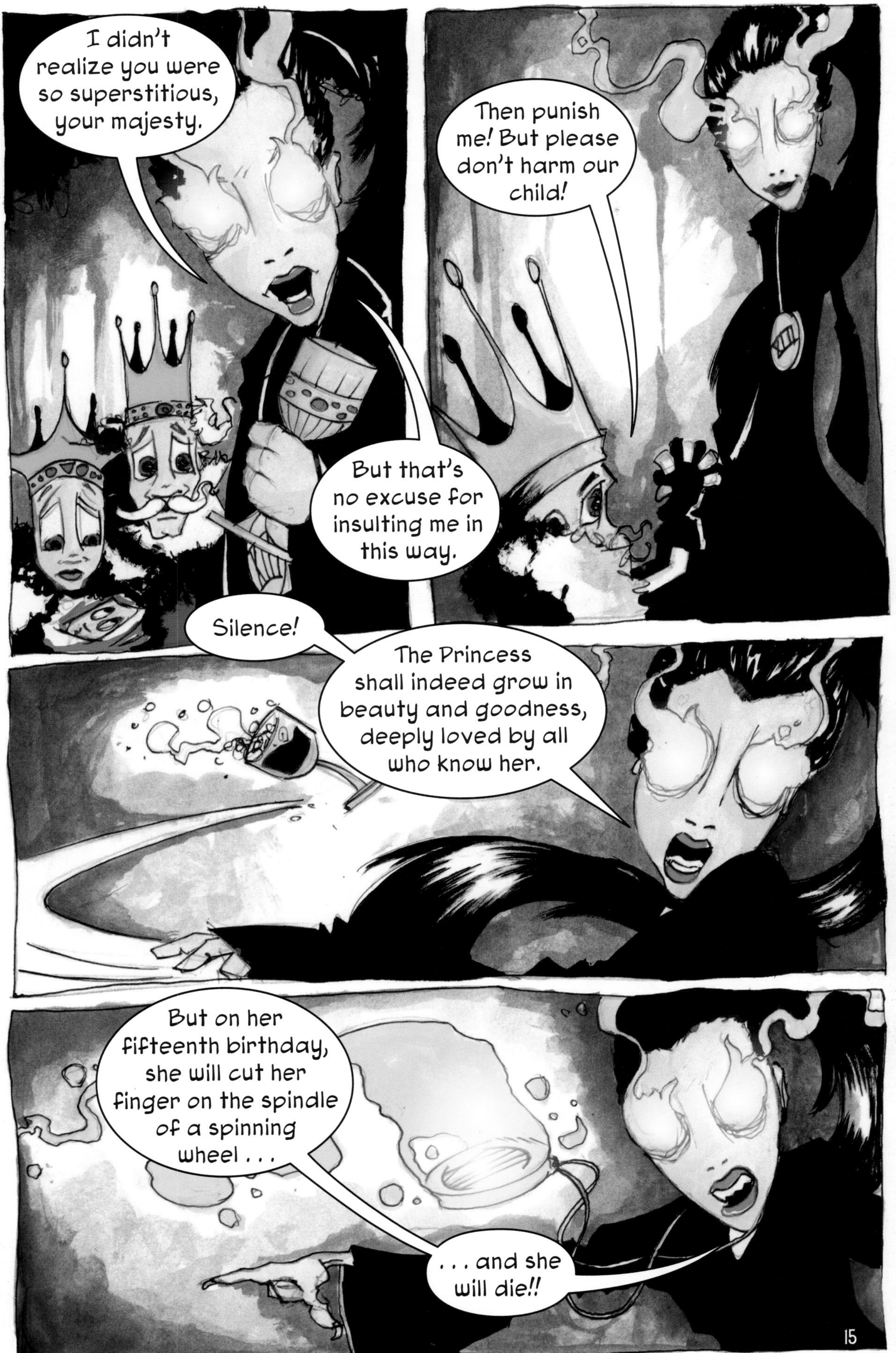
I didn't realize you were so superstitious, your majesty.
But that's no excuse for insulting me in this way.
Then punish me! But please don't harm our child!
Silence!
The Princess shall indeed grow in beauty and goodness, deeply loved by all who know her.
But on her fifteenth birthday, she will cut her finger on the spindle of a spinning wheel . . .
. . . and she will die!!

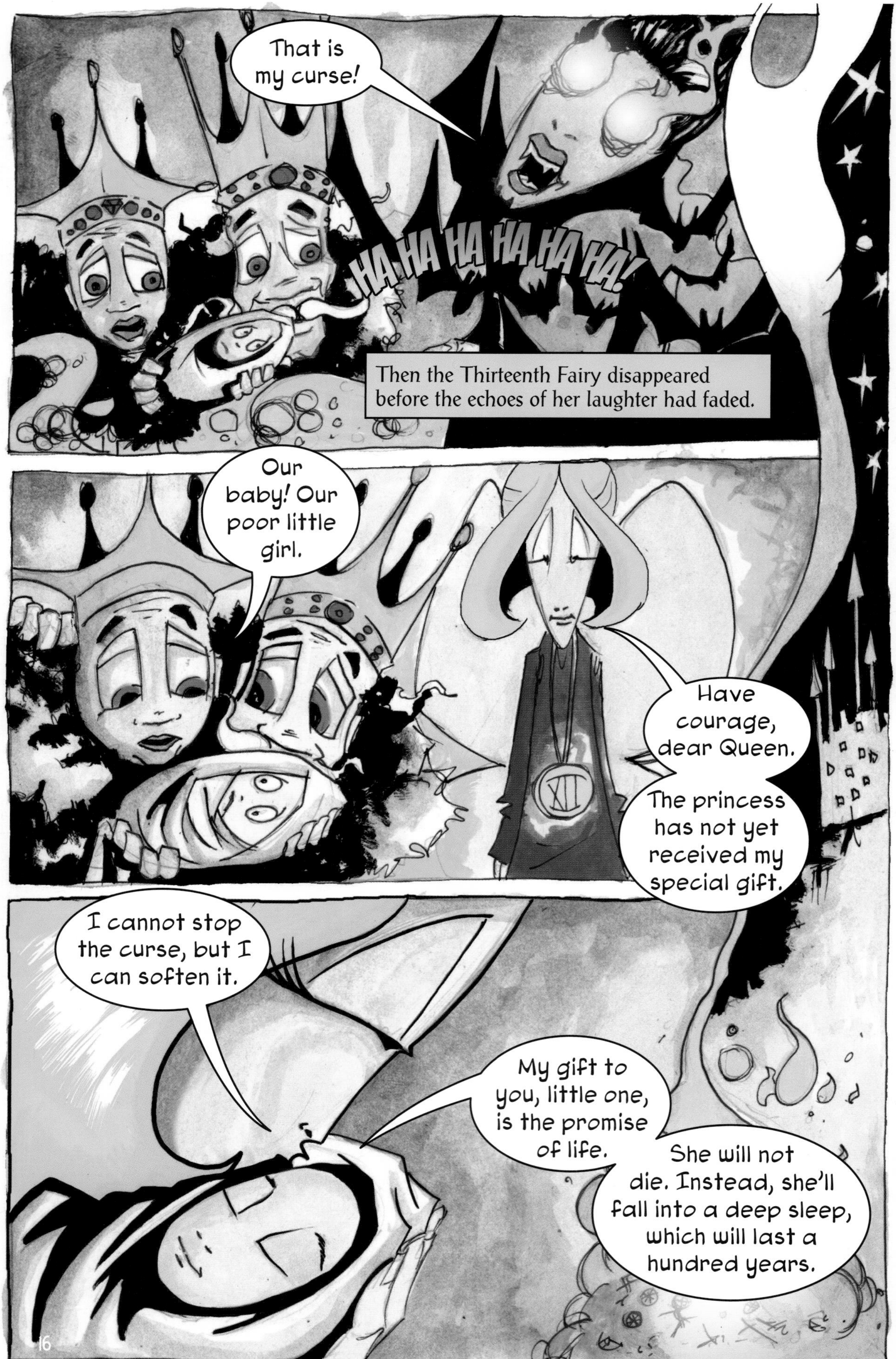
That is my curse!
HA HA HA HA HA HA!
Then the Thirteenth Fairy disappeared before the echoes of her laughter had faded.
Our baby! Our poor little girl.
Have courage, dear Queen.
The princess has not yet received my special gift.
I cannot stop the curse, but I can soften it.
My gift to you, little one, is the promise of life.
She will not die. Instead, she'll fall into a deep sleep, which will last a hundred years.

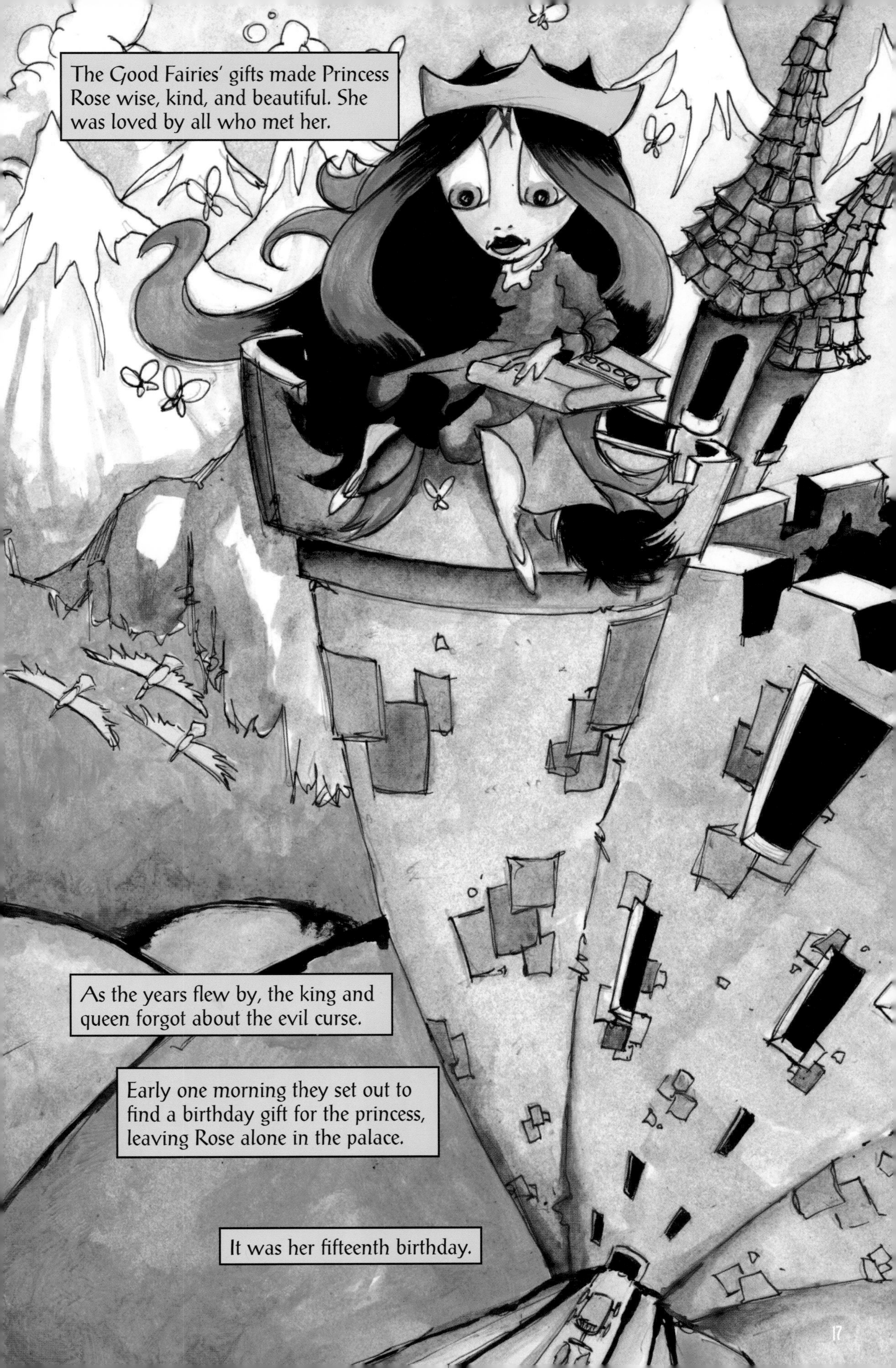
The Good Fairies' gifts made Princess Rose wise, kind, and beautiful. She was loved by all who met her.
As the years flew by, the king and queen forgot about the evil curse.
Early one morning they set out to find a birthday gift for the princess, leaving Rose alone in the palace.
It was her fifteenth birthday.

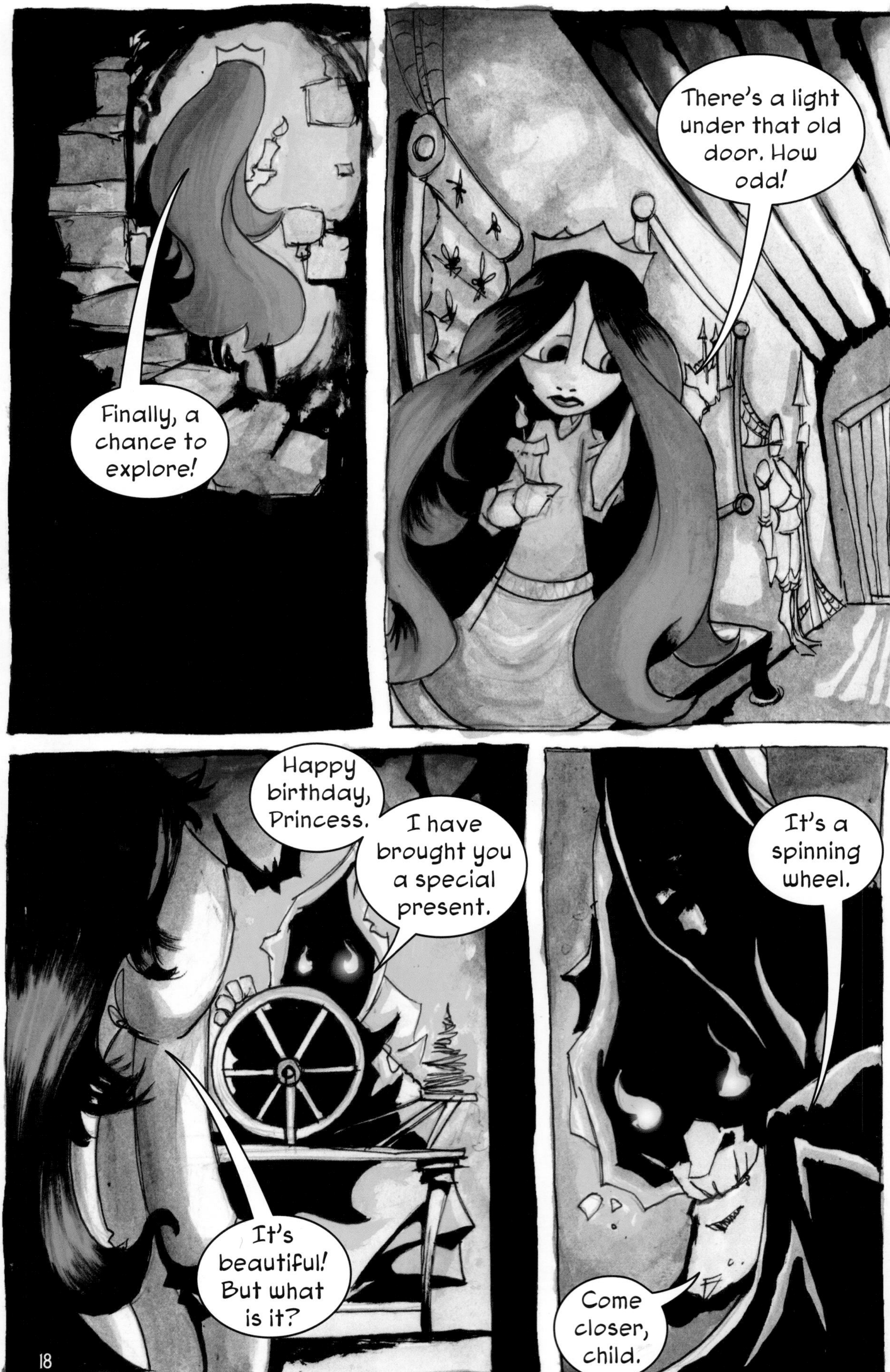
Finally, a chance to explore!
There's a light under that old door. How odd!
Happy birthday, Princess.
I have brought you a special present.
It's beautiful! But what is it?
It's a spinning wheel.
Come closer, child.

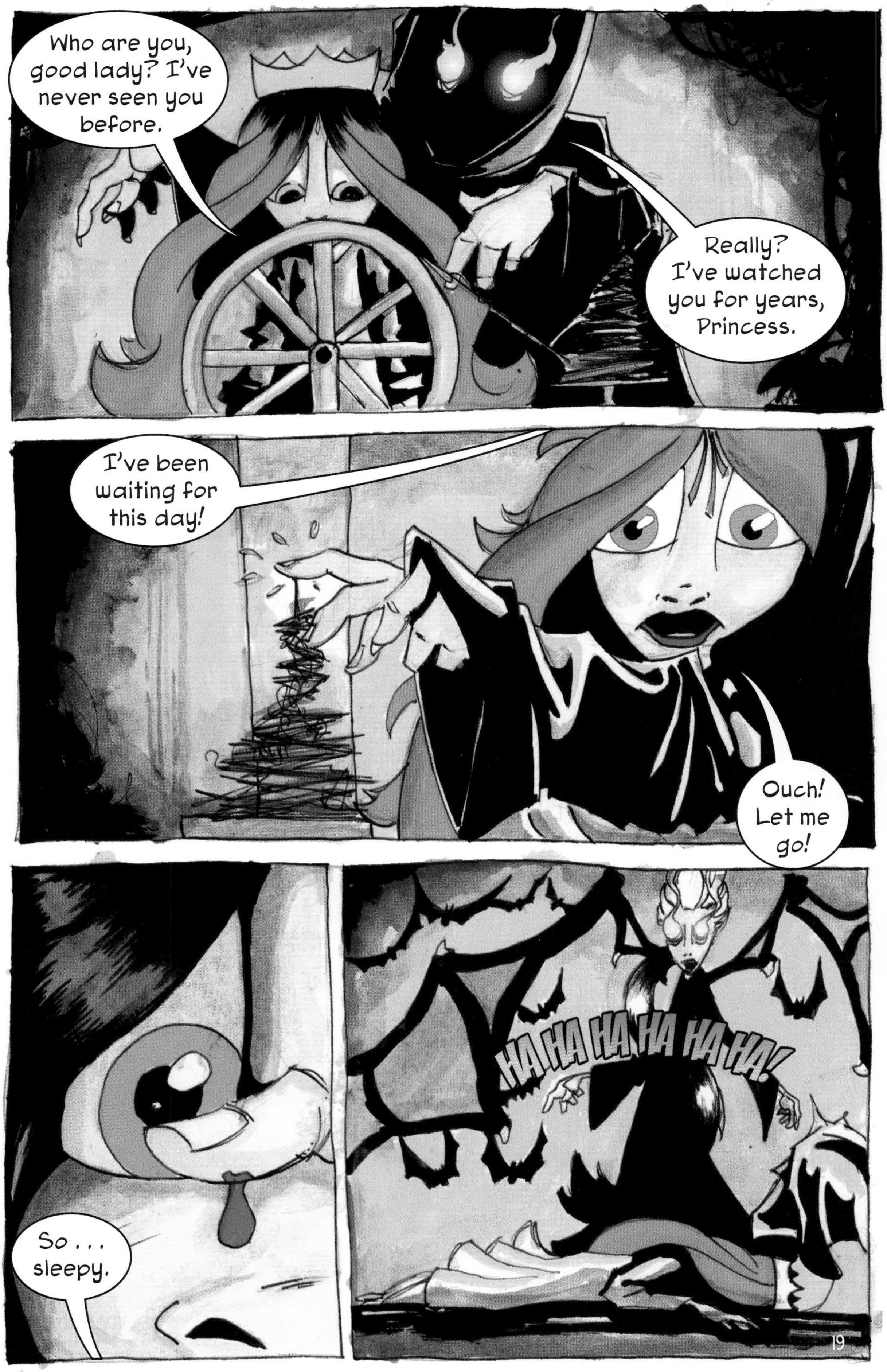

Who are you, good lady? I've never seen you before.
Really? I've watched you for years, Princess.
I've been waiting for this day!
Ouch! Let me go!
So . . . sleepy.
HA HA HA HA HA HA!

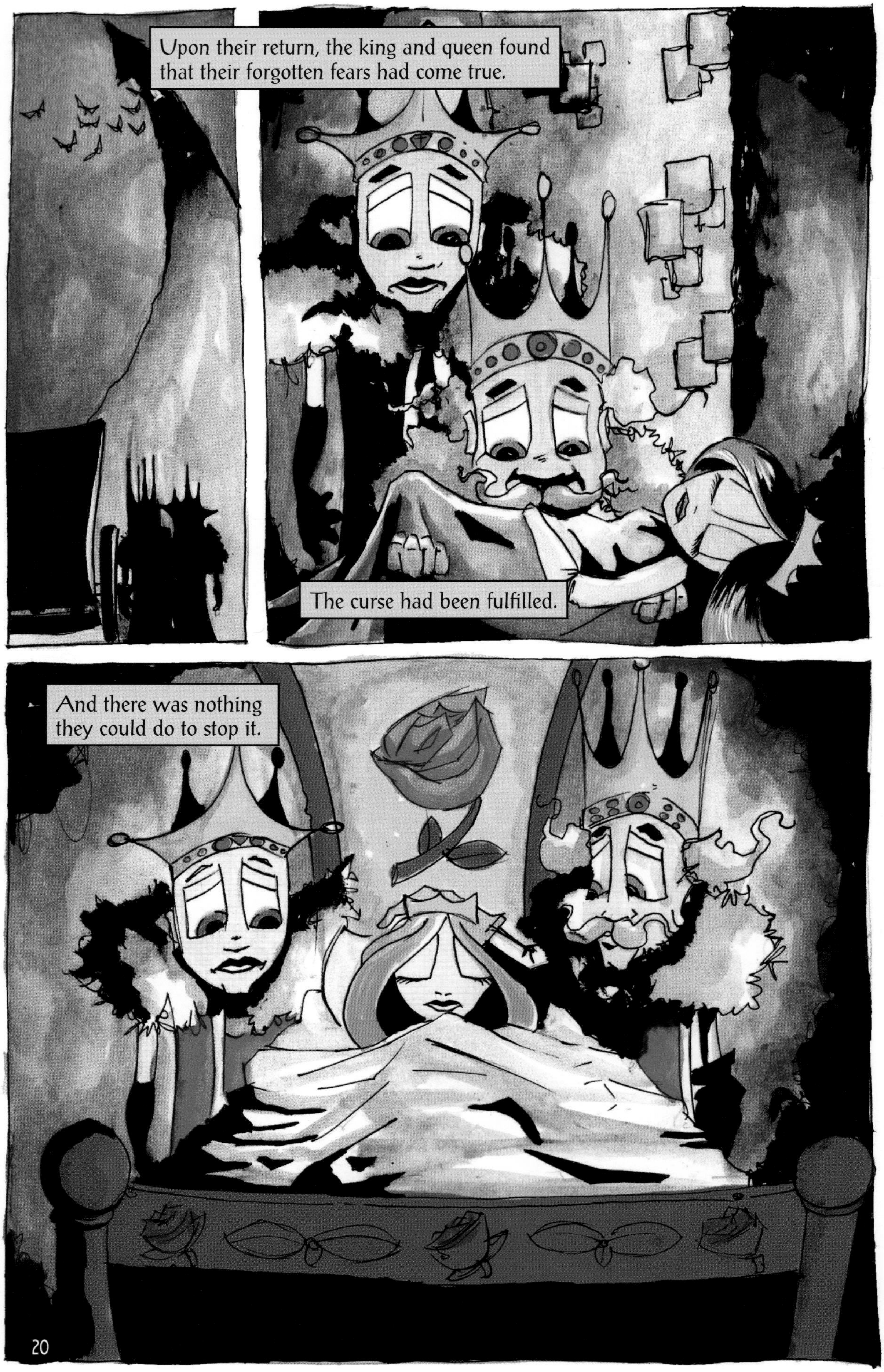
Upon their return, the king and queen found that their forgotten fears had come true.
The curse had been fulfilled.
And there was nothing they could do to stop it.

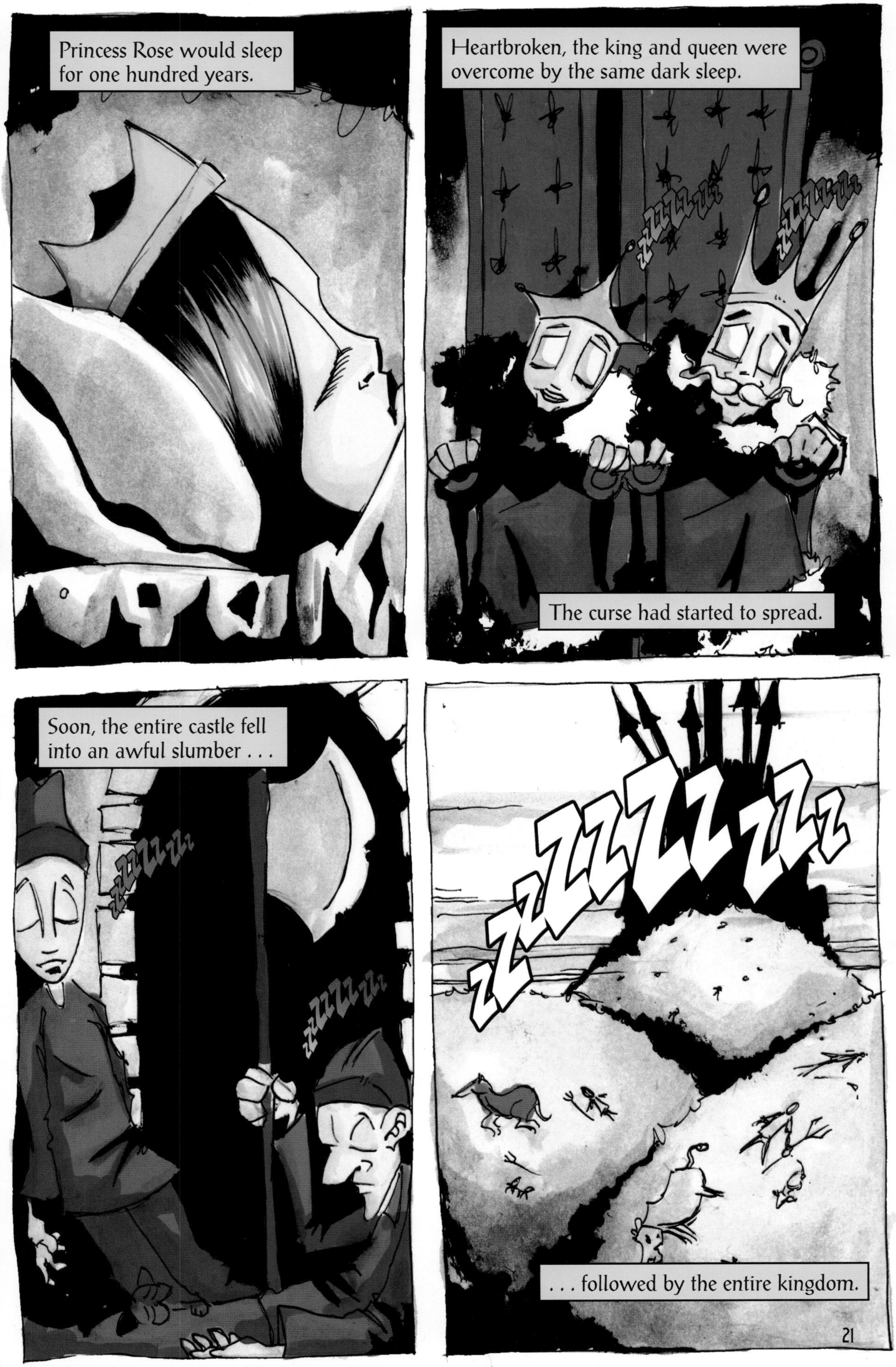
Princess Rose would sleep for one hundred years.
Heartbroken, the king and queen were overcome by the same dark sleep.
The curse had started to spread.
Soon, the entire castle fell into an awful slumber . . .
. . . followed by the entire kingdom.

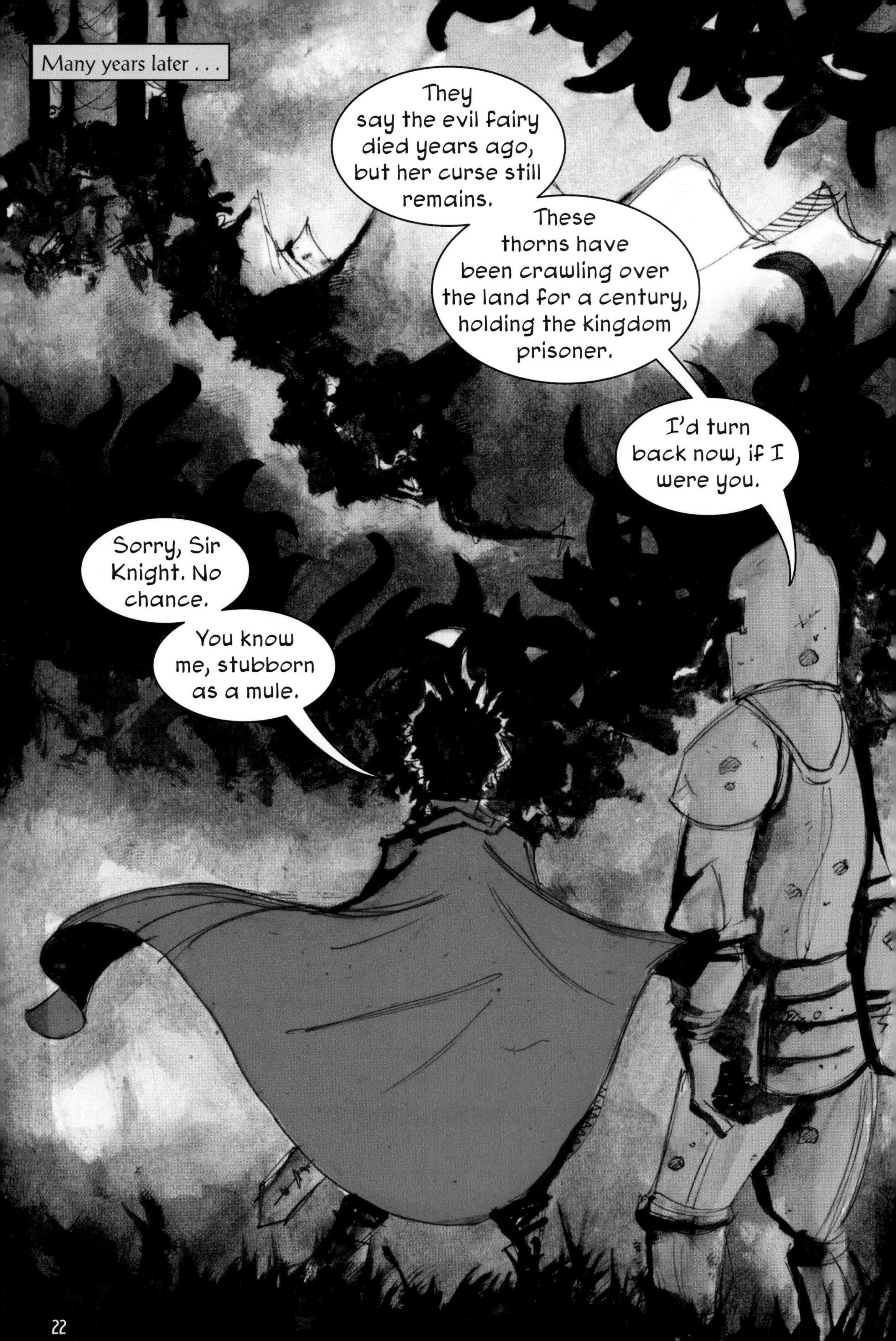
Many years later . . .
They say the evil fairy died years ago, but her curse still remains.
These thorns have been crawling over the land for a century, holding the kingdom prisoner.
I'd turn back now, if I were you.
Sorry, Sir Knight. No chance.
You know me, stubborn as a mule.

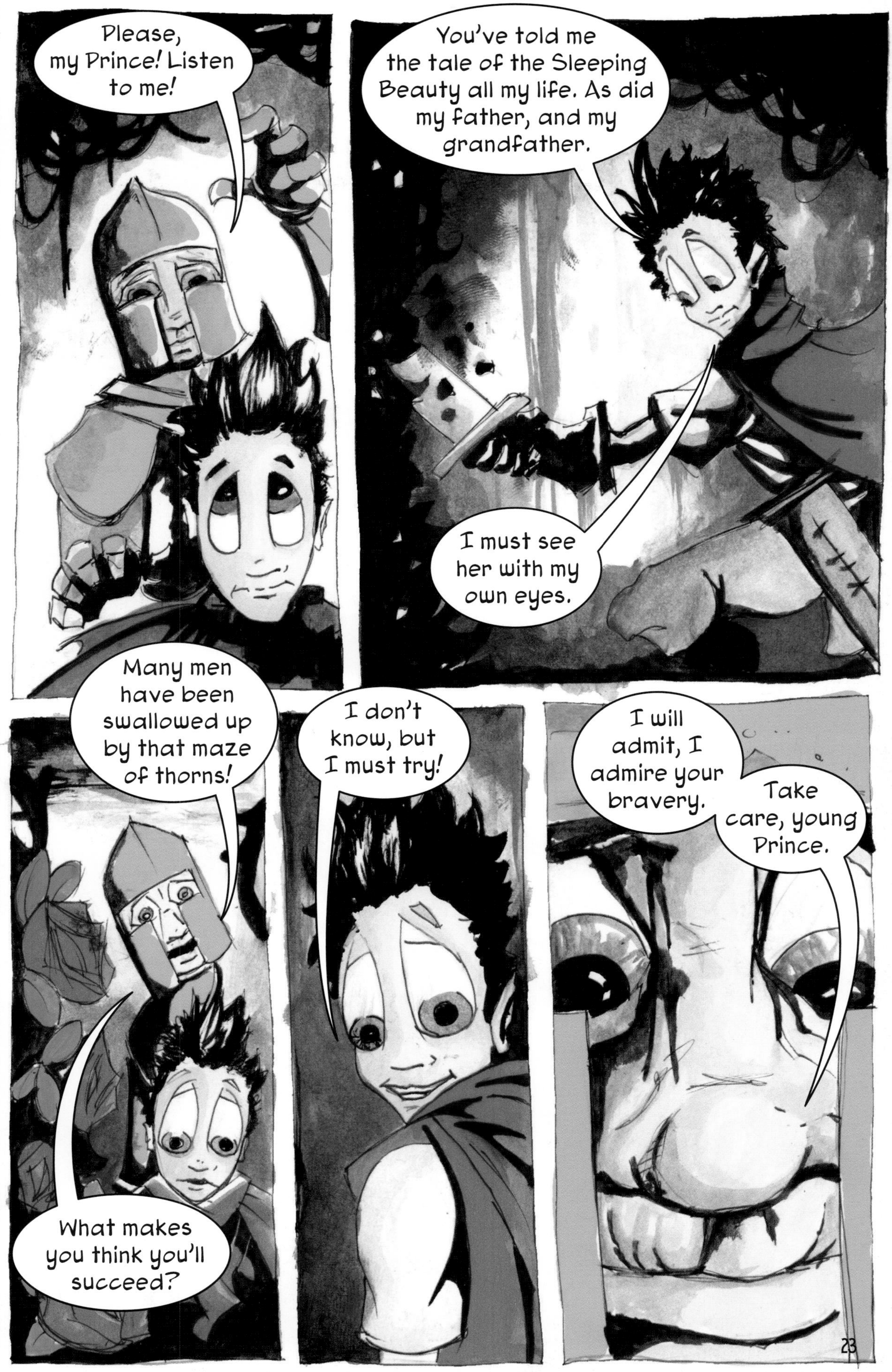
Please, my Prince! Listen to me!
You've told me the tale of the Sleeping Beauty all my life. As did my father, and my grandfather.
I must see her with my own eyes.
Many men have been swallowed up by that maze of thorns!
What makes you think you'll succeed?
I don't know, but I must try!
I will admit, I admire your bravery.
Take care, young Prince.

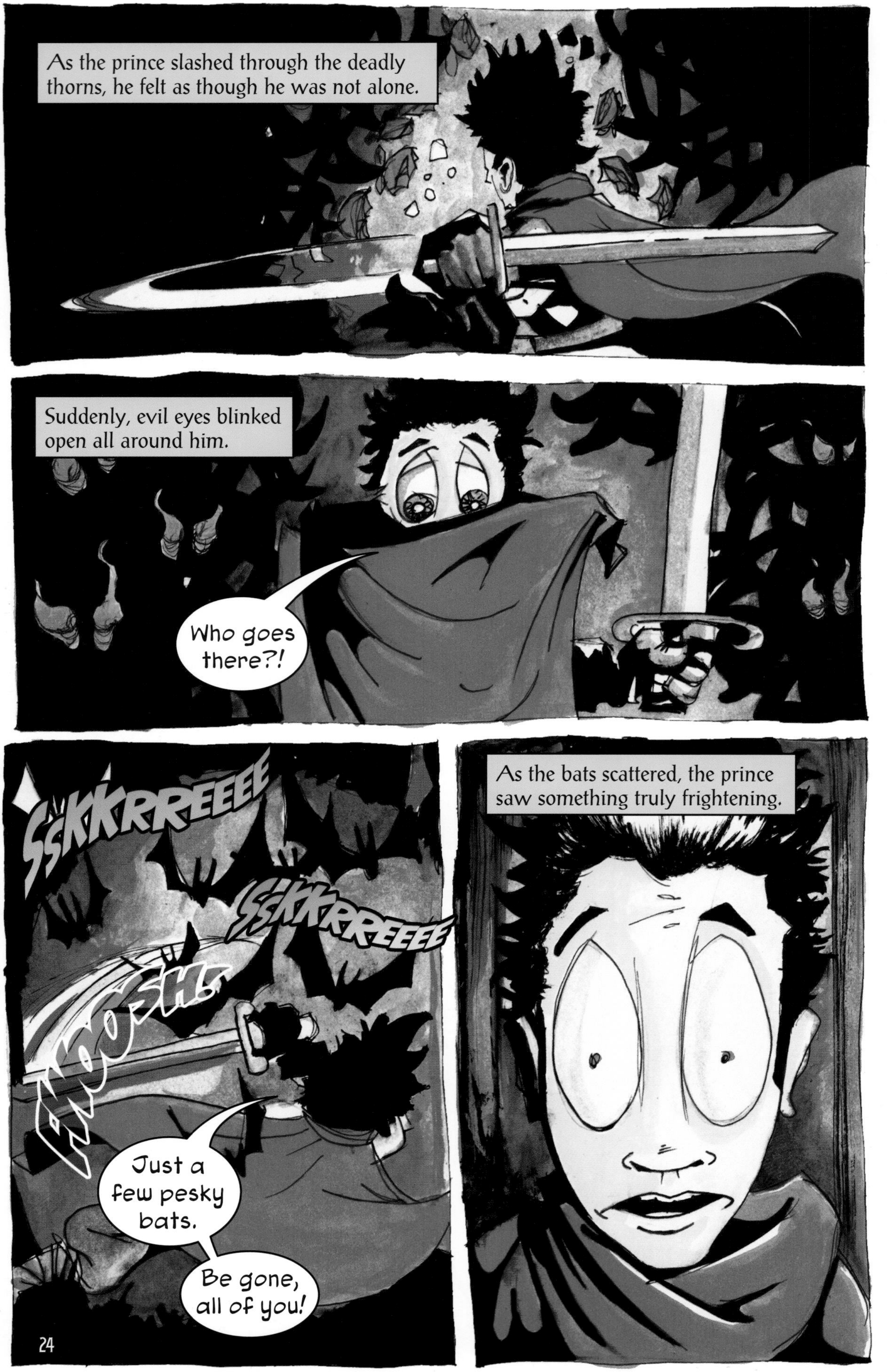
As the prince slashed through the deadly thorns, he felt as though he was not alone.
Suddenly, evil eyes blinked open all around him.
Who goes there?!
SSKKRREEEE
SSKKRREEEE
WHOOSH!
Just a few pesky bats.
Be gone, all of you!
As the bats scattered, the prince saw something truly frightening.

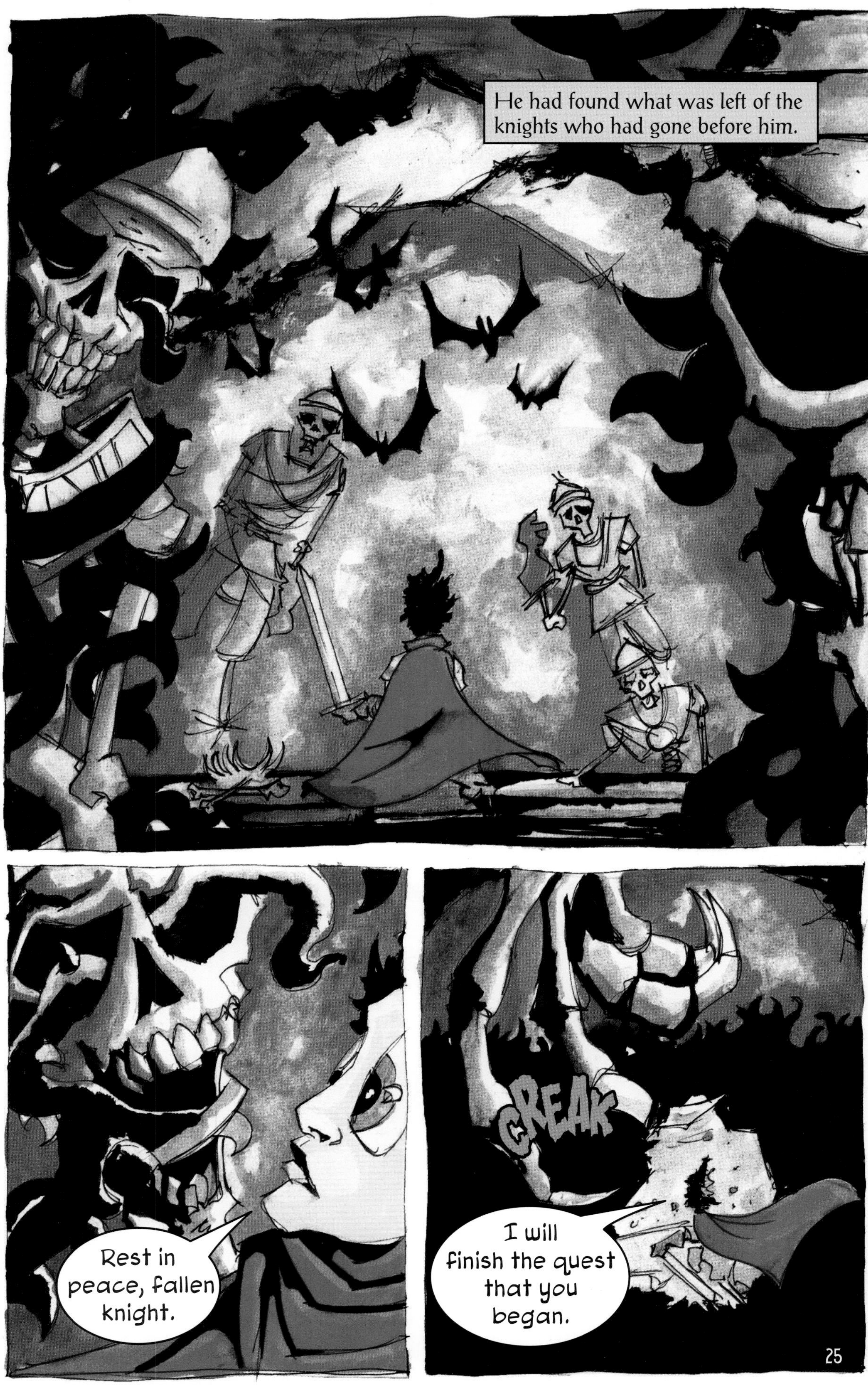
He had found what was left of the knights who had gone before him.
Rest in peace, fallen knight.
CREAK
I will finish the quest that you began.

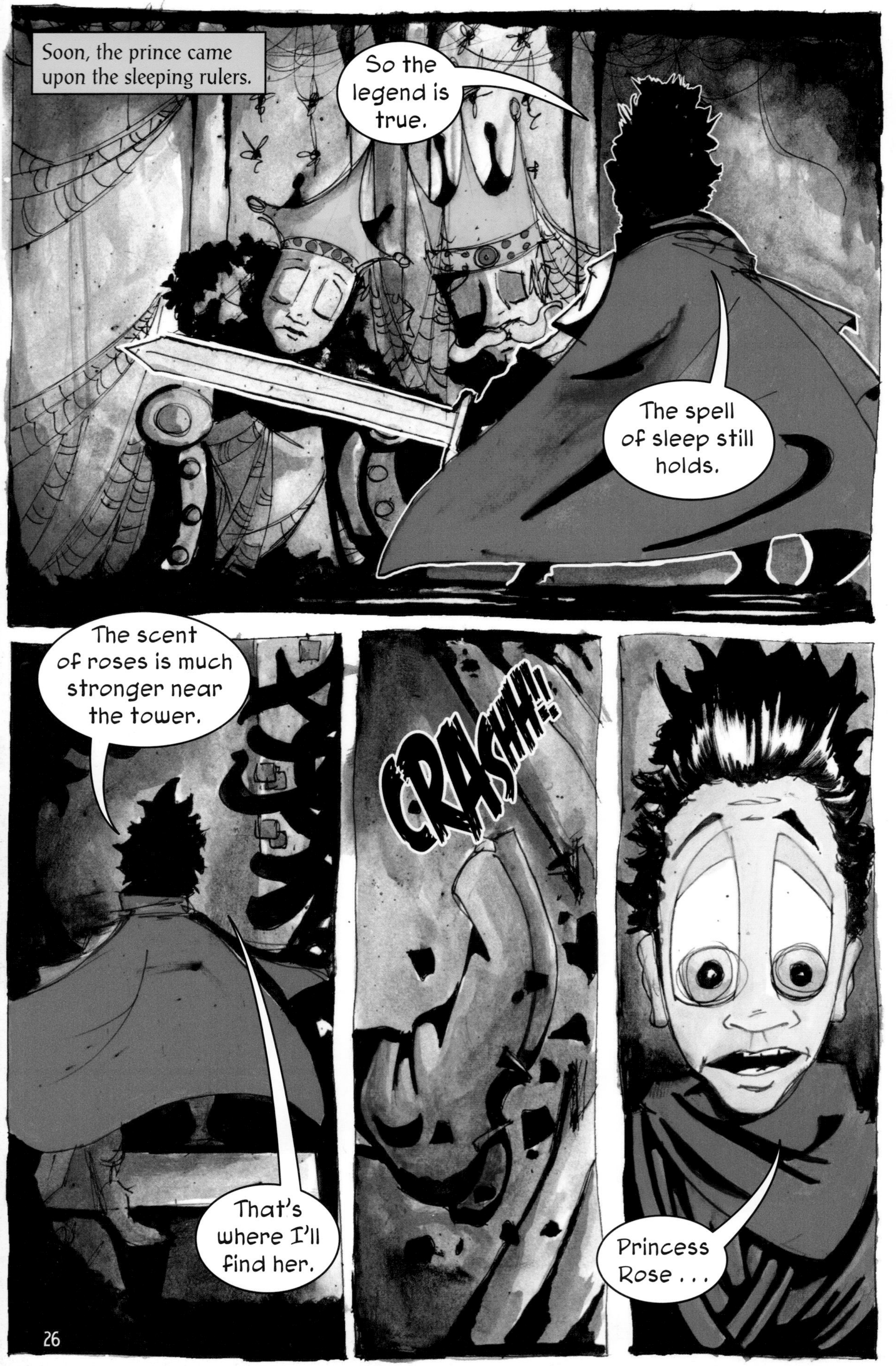
Soon, the prince came upon the sleeping rulers.
So the legend is true.
The spell of sleep still holds.
The scent of roses is much stronger near the tower.
That's where I'll find her.
CRASHH!!
Princess Rose . . .

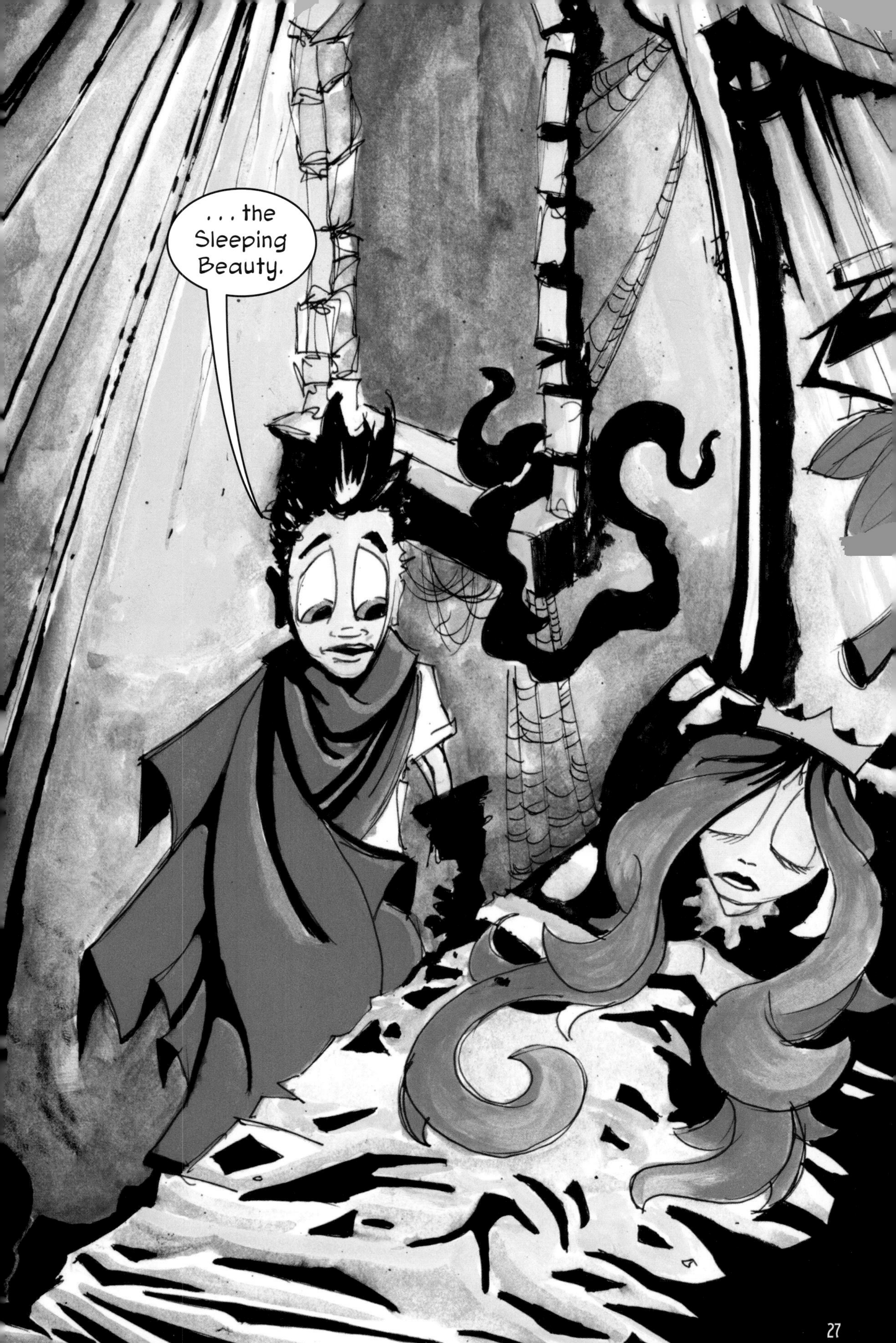
. . . the Sleeping Beauty.

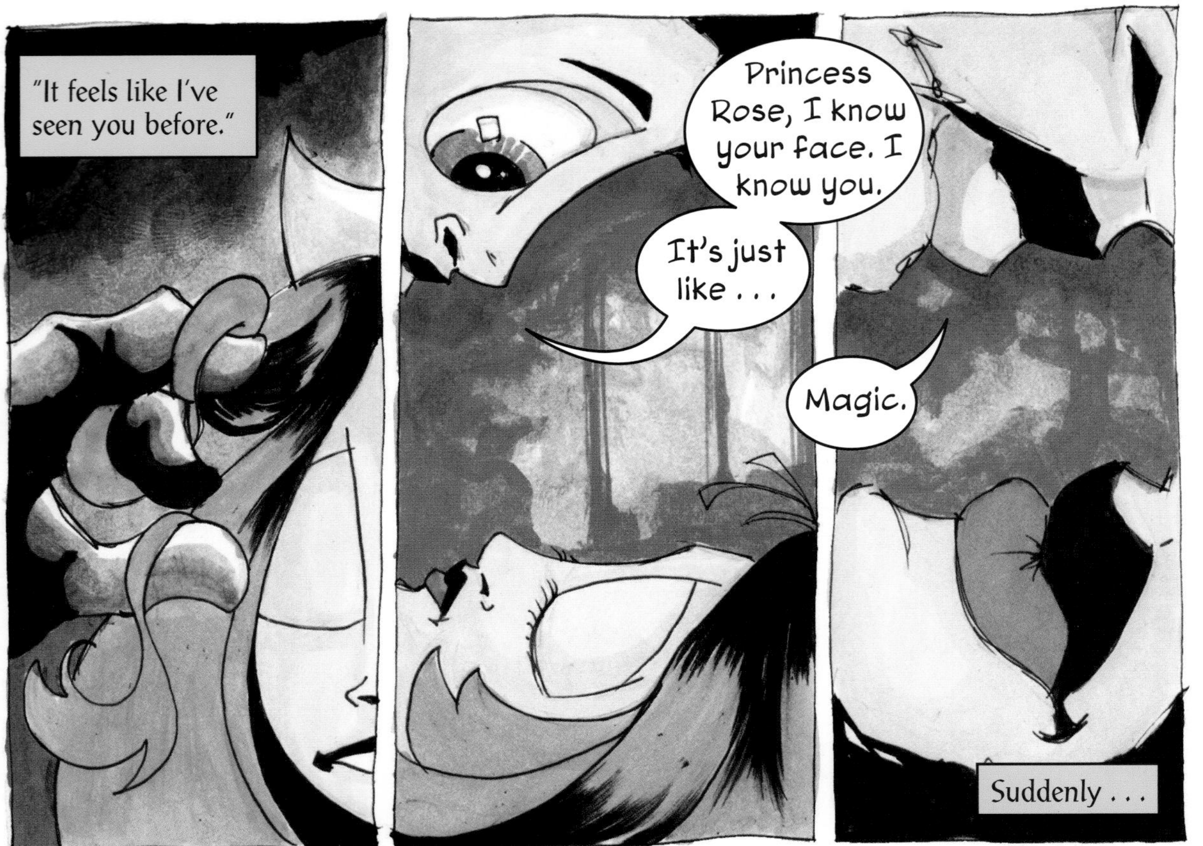
"It feels like I've seen you before."
Princess Rose, I know your face. I know you.
It's just like . . .
Magic.
Suddenly . . .

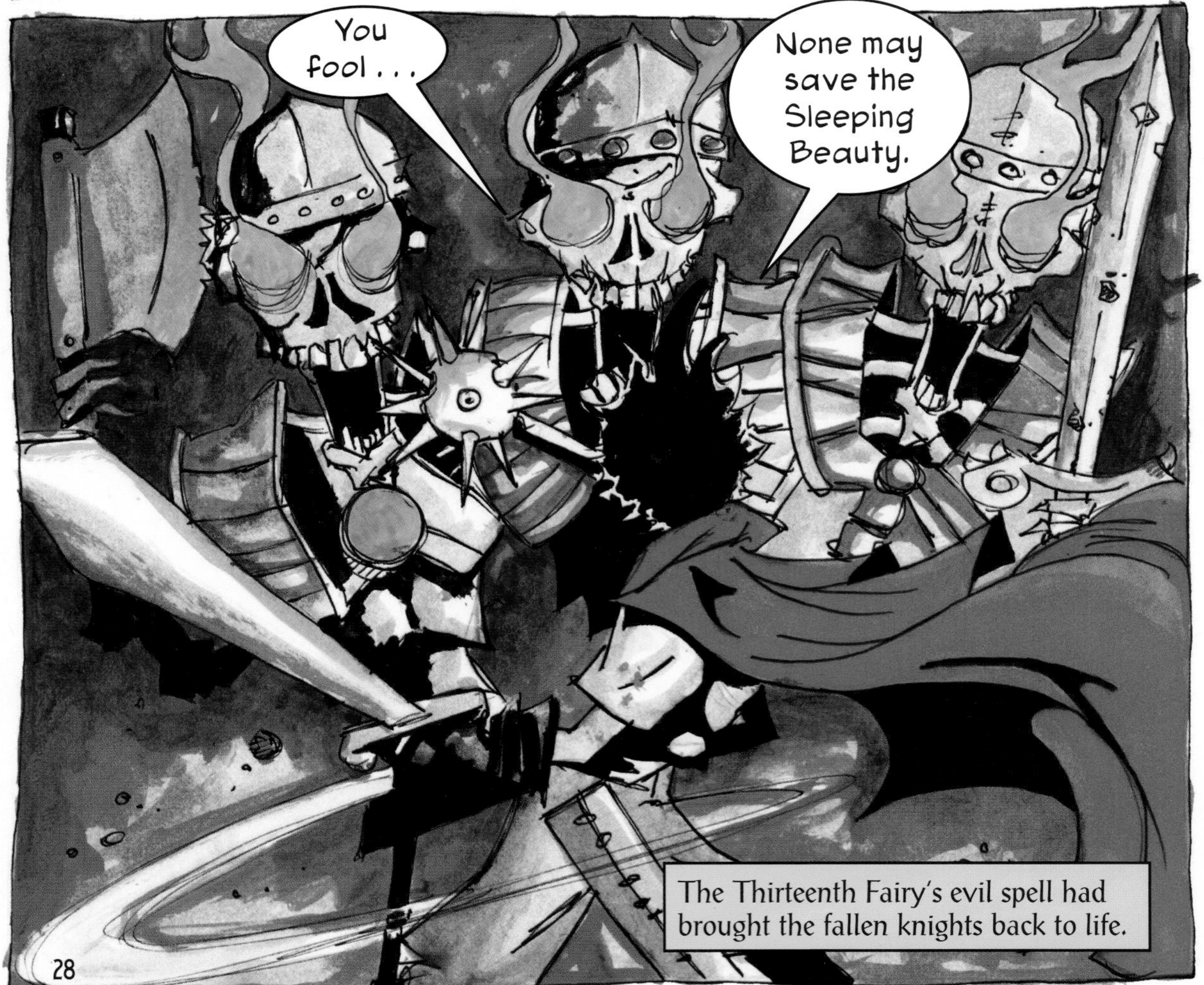
You fool . . .
None may save the Sleeping Beauty.
The Thirteenth Fairy's evil spell had brought the fallen knights back to life.

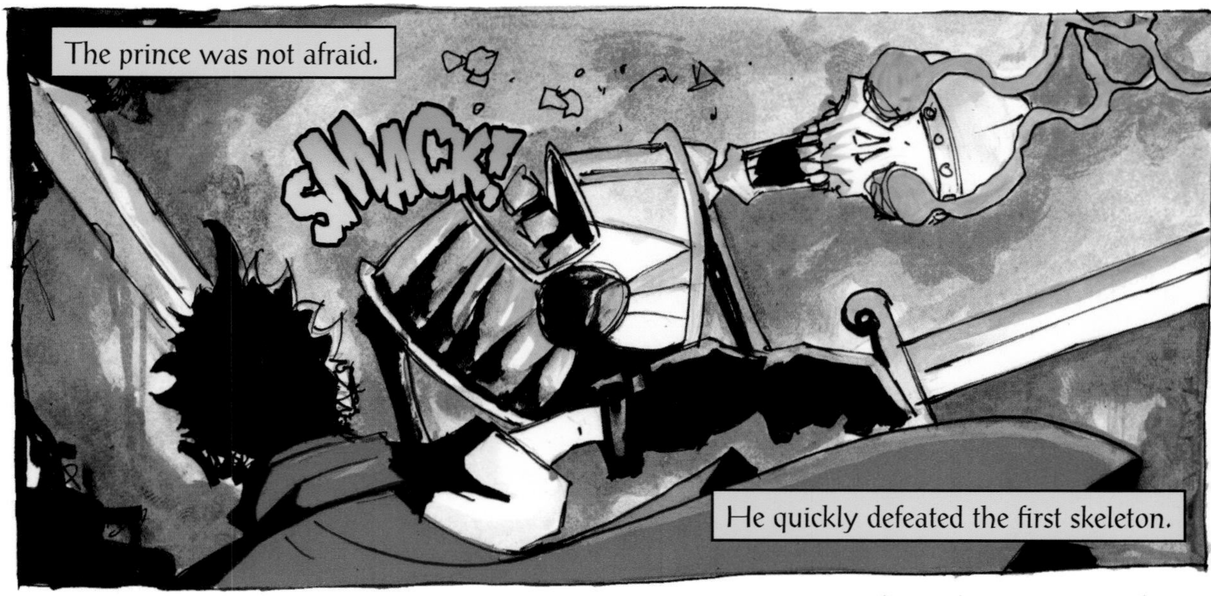
The prince was not afraid.
SMACK!
He quickly defeated the first skeleton.

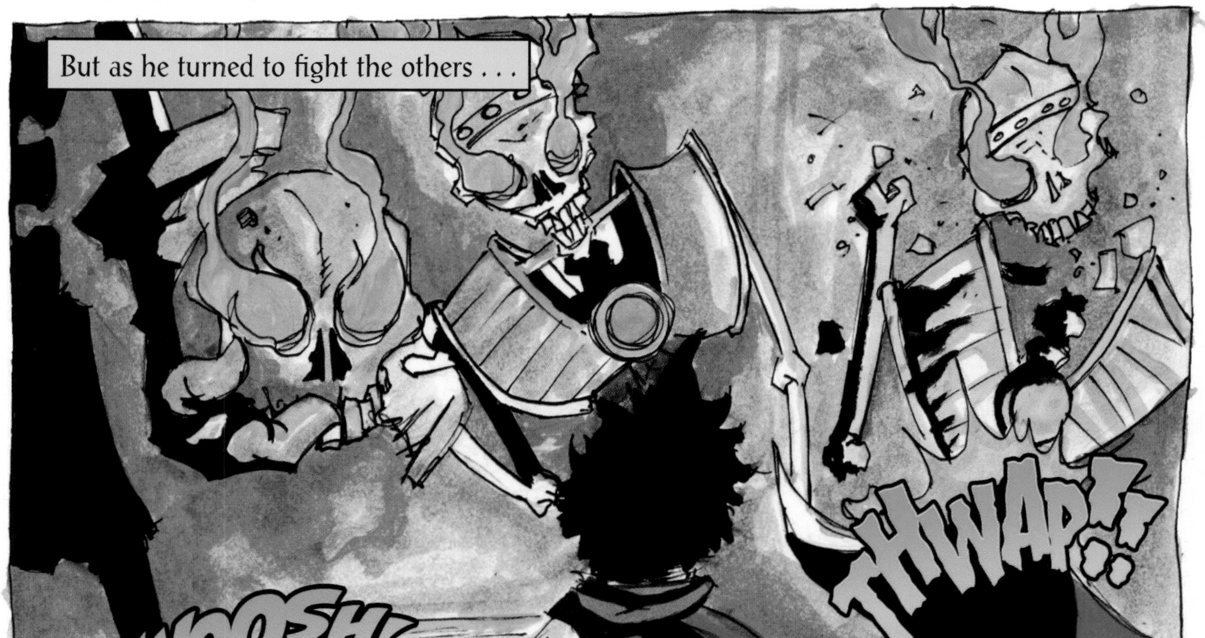
But as he turned to fight the others . . .
THWAP!!
SWOOSH!
. . . a mighty blow sent him flying through the window.

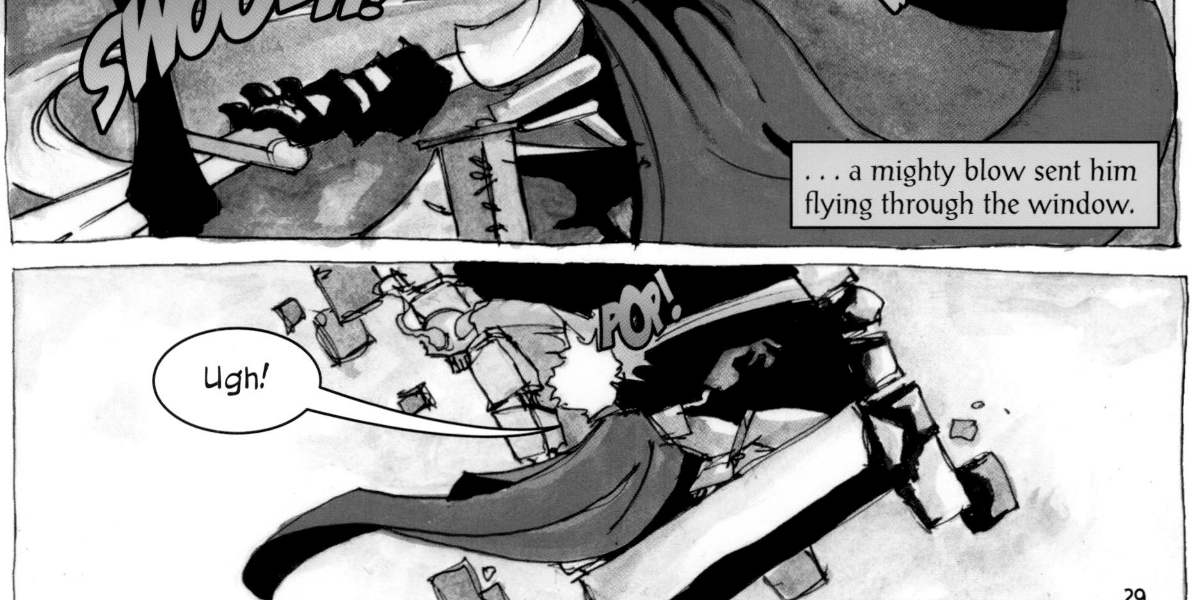
POP!
Ugh!

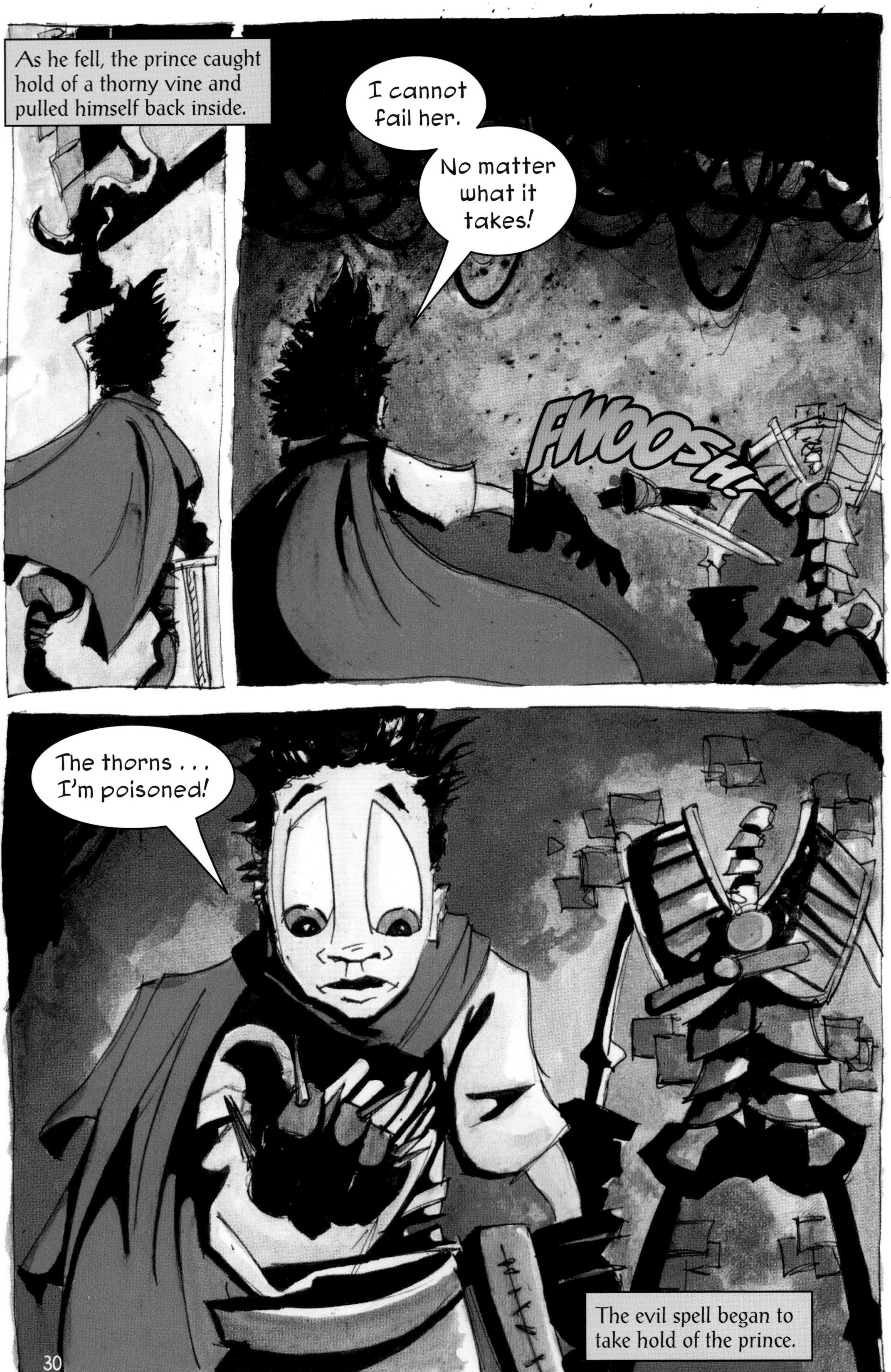
As he fell, the prince caught hold of a thorny vine and pulled himself back inside.
I cannot fail her.
No matter what it takes!
FWOOSH!
The thorns . . . I'm poisoned!
The evil spell began to take hold of the prince.

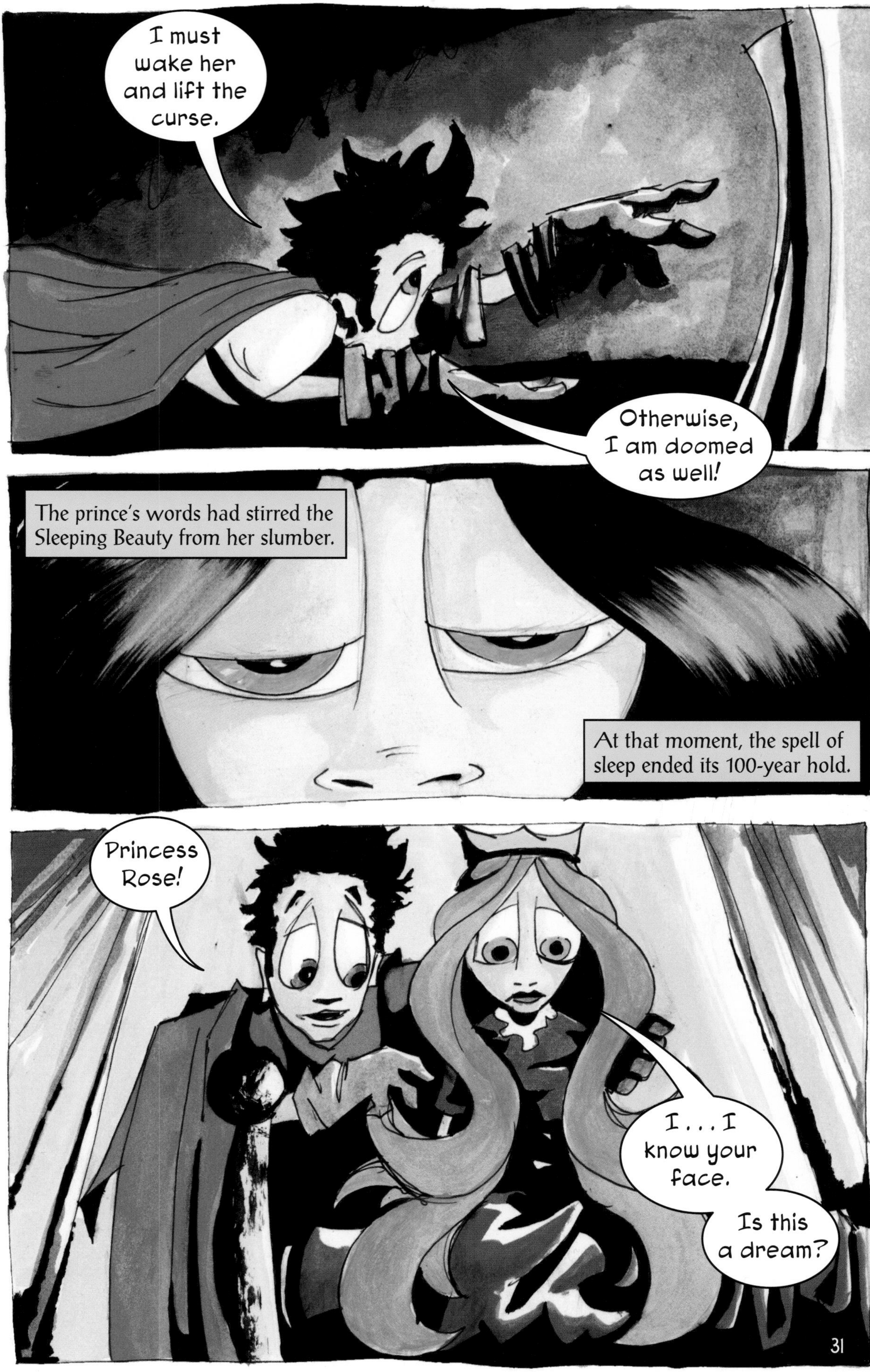
I must wake her and lift the curse.
Otherwise, I am doomed as well!
The prince's words had stirred the Sleeping Beauty from her slumber.
At that moment, the spell of sleep ended its 100-year hold.
Princess Rose!
I . . . I know your face.
Is this a dream?

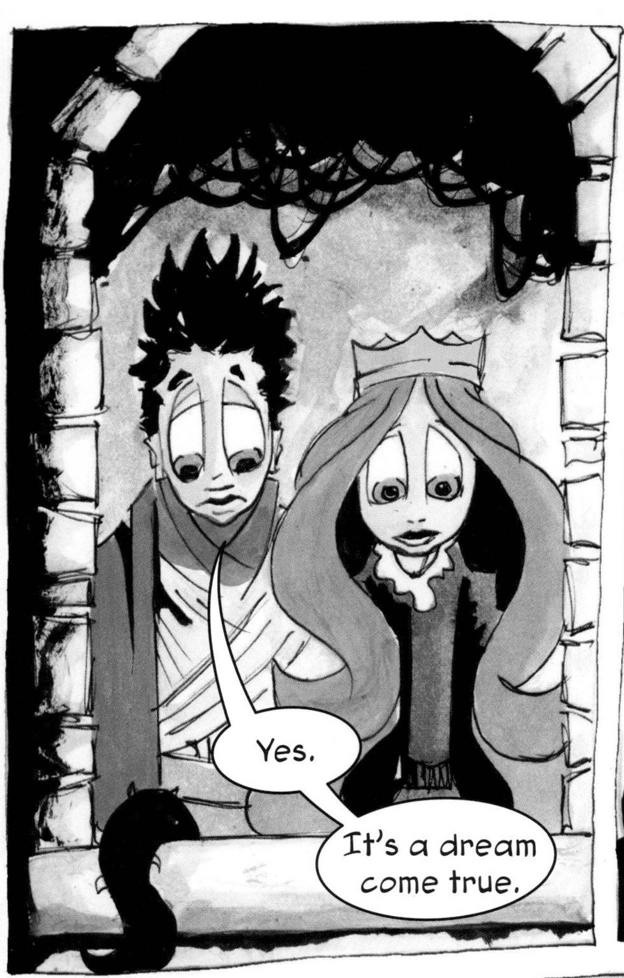
Yes.
It's a dream come true.

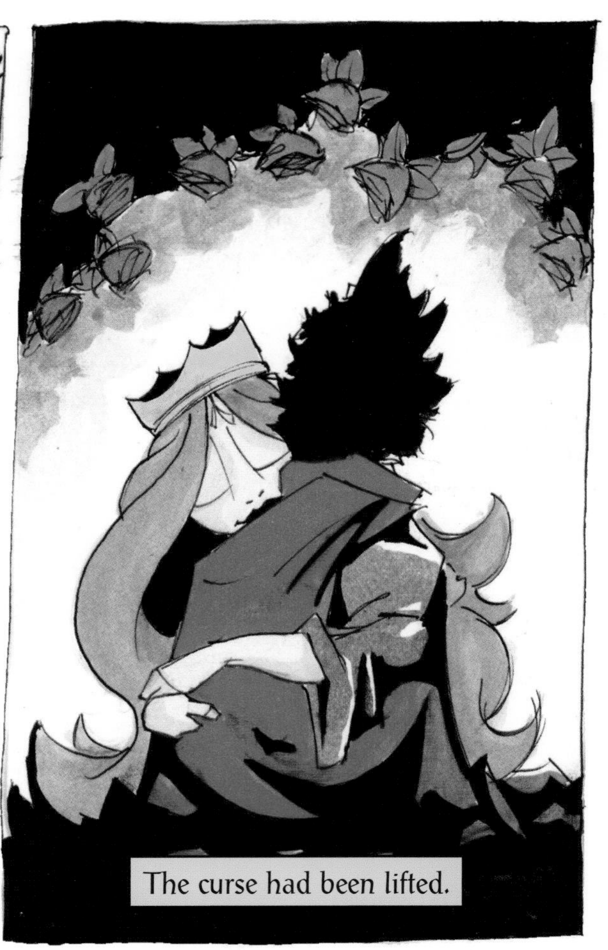
The curse had been lifted.

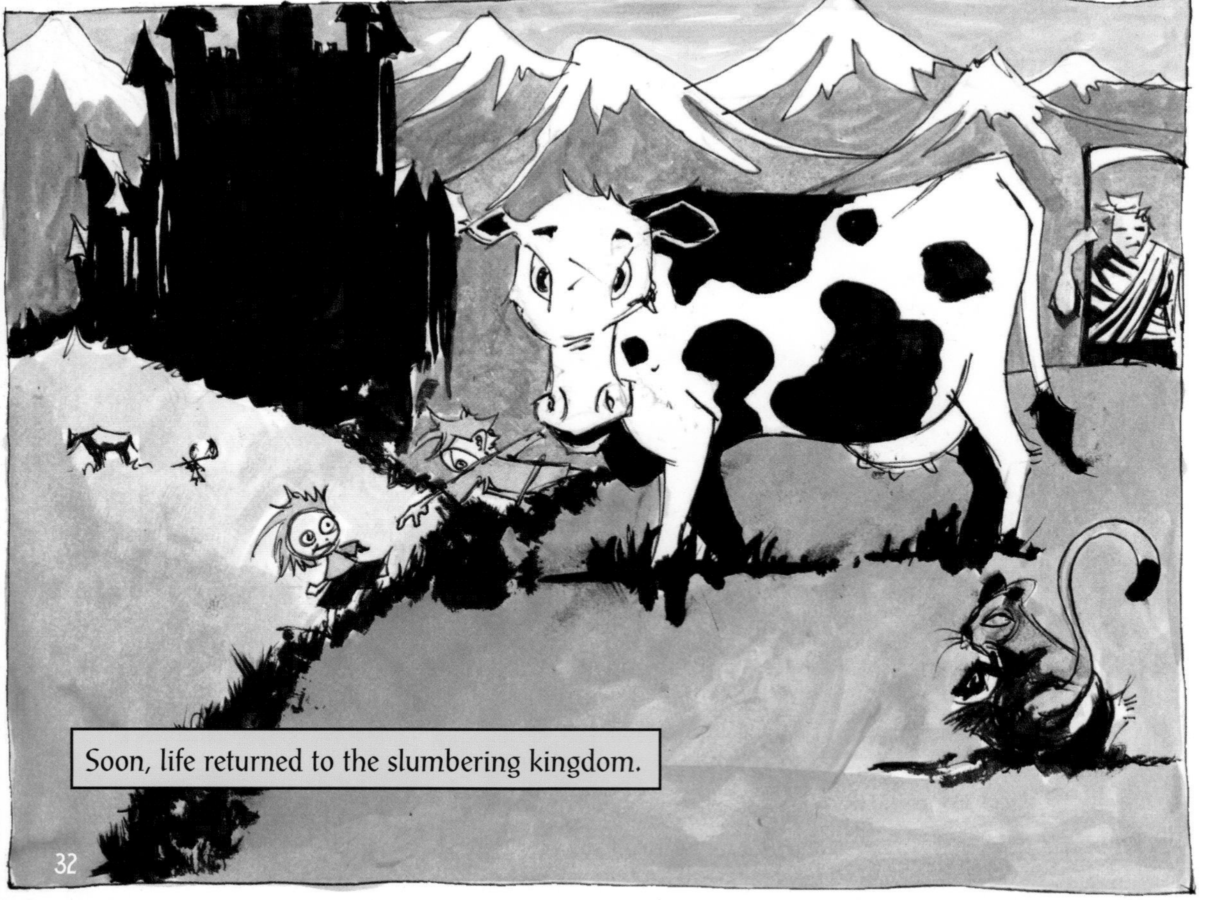
Soon, life returned to the slumbering kingdom.

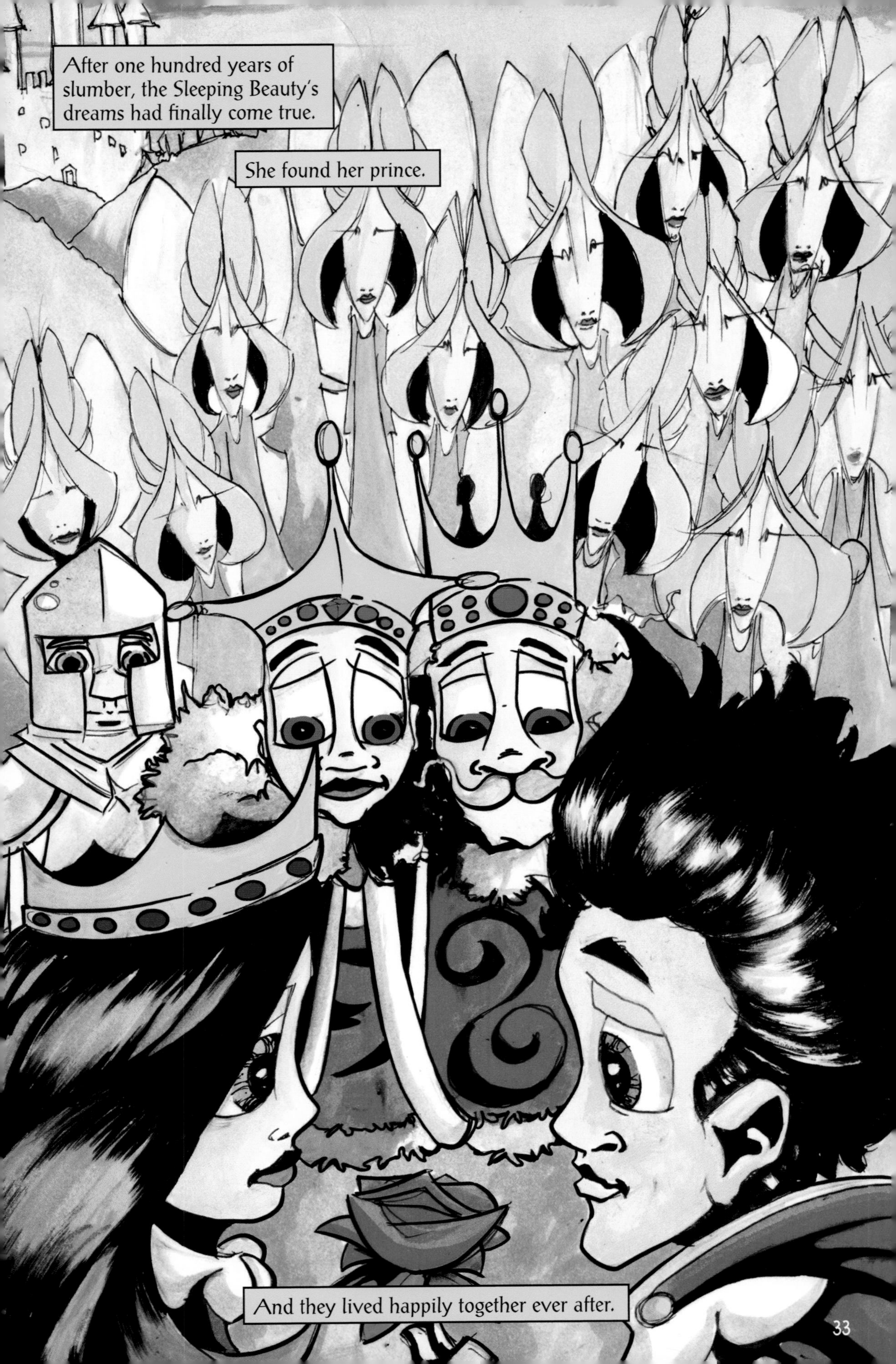
After one hundred years of slumber, the Sleeping Beauty's dreams had finally come true.
She found her prince.
And they lived happily together ever after.

ABOUT THE AUTHOR

Since 1986, Martin Powell has been a freelance writer. He has written hundreds of stories, many of which have been published by Disney, Marvel, Tekno Comix, Moonstone Books, and others. In 1989, Powell received an Eisner Award nomination for his graphic novel *Scarlet in Gaslight*. This award is one of the highest comic book honors.

ABOUT THE ILLUSTRATOR

Sean Dietrich was born in Baltimore, Maryland, and now lives in San Diego, California. He's been drawing since the age of 4. He had his first art show at age 6, self-published his first comic book at 16, and has won more than 53 art awards throughout the years. When he's not drawing, Dietrich says he spends too much time in front of the TV playing video games.

GLOSSARY

curse (KURSS)—an evil spell intended to harm someone

desire (di-ZIRE)—a strong wish or need for something or someone

legend (LEJ-uhnd)—a story handed down from earlier times

modesty (MOD-iss-tee)—people who are modest do not brag about their abilities or possessions

spindle (SPIN-duhl)—the rod on a spinning wheel that holds or winds thread

stubborn (STUHB-urn)—not willing to change

superstitious (soo-pur-STI-shuhs)—believing that some things are lucky or unlucky

THE HISTORY OF
SLEEPING BEAUTY

Like so many fairy tales, the story of Sleeping Beauty was first an oral tale. In 1697, a French author, Charles Perrault, published a collection of these oral fairy tales. His book included "Little Red Riding Hood," "Cinderella," and of course, "The Sleeping Beauty in the Wood."

Perrault's story included a second part, which takes place after the prince wakes Sleeping Beauty. The happy pair are married and have two children. But the prince keeps his marriage a secret from his mother, who is an ogress. After he takes the throne, the prince brings his family to the castle. When he is called away to war, his monster mother makes plans to eat her daughter-in-law and grandchildren. The prince returns just in time. His mother throws herself in a pit of snakes, and the rest of the family is free to live happily ever after.

Sleeping Beauty is the theme of a famous Russian ballet composed by Pyotr Tchaikovsky in 1890. Tchaikovsky's music was also used in the Walt Disney movie version of the fairy tale. The 1959 film took five years to animate. It cost $6 million dollars to make, but the film earned only $3 million when it hit theaters. Today, however, *Sleeping Beauty* is considered one of Disney's classics.

DISCUSSION QUESTIONS

1. Pretend you are one of the fairies who grants a gift to the baby princess. What gift would you give the princess and why?

2. Imagine everyone in your school fell asleep for a hundred years, just like the kingdom in the story. How would life be different when you all woke up?

3. Fairy tales are often told over and over again. Have you heard the "Sleeping Beauty" fairy tale before? How is this version of the story different from other versions you've heard, seen, or read?

WRITING PROMPTS

1. Fairy tales are fantasy stories, often about wizards, goblins, giants, and fairies. Many fairy tales have a happy ending. Write your own fairy tale. Then read it to a friend or family member.

2. Write a new version of "Sleeping Beauty" with a different curse. Maybe Sleeping Beauty becomes Dancing Beauty, a girl who cannot stop dancing for 10 years. What curse can you think up?

3. Imagine that someone else woke Sleeping Beauty before the prince had a chance. What if a silly old woman woke her up by vacuuming? Or perhaps a little boy tickled her with a feather. Write the wake-up scene between this new character and Sleeping Beauty.

INTERNET SITES

The book may be over, but the adventure is just beginning.

Do you want to read more about the subjects or ideas in this book? Want to play cool games or watch videos about the authors who write these books? Then go to FactHound. At www.facthound.com, you'll be able to do all that, and more. The FactHound website can also send you to other safe Internet sites.

Check it out!